"IT'S THE GUN THAT KILLED ELIZABETH!" BRYAN WHISPERED. "Dusty thinks I shot her." Suddenly he keeled over. Meg stared astonished at him lying limply on top of the gun. "B-Bryan?" For one horrible instant she thought he was dead, but when she knelt beside him, she saw that he was breathing.

A noise came from the direction of the boat. Meg leapt up suddenly and the flashlight fell to the floor with a clatter and flickered off. She stood very still, straining her ears, but all she could hear was the drumming of a few raindrops on the roof of the boat house. She held her breath, suddenly aware of the profound darkness. She couldn't see anything, neither Bryan nor the boat. Damp air blew in from the open doorway, but the square of dim light she expected to see wasn't there. She inched backward slowly and jumped when she heard another scraping sound and then a bump. Someone else was in the boat house!

Books by Janice Harrell

Flashpoint
The Murder Game

Available from ARCHWAY Paperbacks

THE MURDER GAME

JANICE HARRELL

AN ARCHWAY PAPERBACK
Published by POCKET BOOKS

New York   London   Toronto   Sydney   Tokyo   Singapore

An ARCHWAY PAPERBACK *Original*

An Archway Paperback published by
POCKET BOOKS, a division of Simon & Schuster Inc.
1230 Avenue of the Americas, New York, NY 10020

Copyright © 1993 by Janice Harrell

ISBN: 0-671-78541-9

First Archway Paperback printing June 1993

10 9 8 7 6 5 4 3 2 1

AN ARCHWAY PAPERBACK and colophon are registered trademarks of Simon & Schuster Inc.

Cover art by Broeck Steadman

Printed in the U.S.A.

IL 6+

THE MURDER GAME

C. C. Carmody finished her test and shook open the school newspaper to the personals column.

"You're invited to an all-night murder. Fun, games, food, no chaperons, no curfew. It'll be a blast. You know who you are—C.C.C., M.R., B.W., K.J., R.B., and J.H. Ask D.E. for details."

C.C. adjusted an earring and reread the ad thoughtfully. She had no trouble deciphering it. Dusty Ellis was having a party, one of those murder game parties like Jeff Holloman had had the year before, with a designated corpse—and she was invited. Her kind of party, too—no chaperons.

It must be about time for Dusty's birthday, she thought. That was right—he and Elizabeth had had their birthday in October. Because they had been premature and were twins, their parents held them back a year in kindergarten. They had been the first in the junior class to get their drivers' licenses. The bit about "no chaperons" probably explained why Dusty had put the ad in the school paper instead of sending invitations. He wouldn't want to risk somebody's mother opening an invitation and putting a stop to the party. C.C. circled the ad in blue marker and slipped the newspaper to Meg Redding, who barely glanced at it. She was busy double-checking her algebra test. That was Meg all over, thought C.C., annoyed. Meg actually carried Band-Aids and a quarter for emergency phone calls in her pocketbook. It was just like her to check her answers when something more exciting was going on. Her auburn hair fell forward and hid her face as she methodically ran down each column of problems. The bell buzzed, and both girls leapt up from their desks and began moving out of the classroom.

"So Dusty's having a party?" said C.C.

Meg flushed. "I guess." She slapped her test down on Mr. Hyatt's desk and rushed out of the classroom as if she were trying to escape.

"Well, either he is having a party or he isn't." C.C. caught up with her. "Hey, is everything okay between you and Dusty? Is anything wrong?"

"Everything's fine. Me and Dusty are fine. I just don't think this party is such a great idea, that's all."

Meg and C.C. had known each other since they were four, and even though they didn't have anything in common anymore, Meg supposed they were still friends. But these days Meg was embarrassed to be seen with C.C., who looked almost like a pirate with her big hoop earrings and short dark hair tucked behind her ears. All she needed to complete the illusion was a black eye patch.

C.C.'s jeans were so tight and so badly torn they were hardly decent. And as for her personal life, it more and more resembled one of the case studies that Meg's psychologist father had on file at his office. C.C. was the only girl Meg knew who had shown up at the junior-senior prom with a thirty-year-old tennis bum.

"It's probably good Dusty's having this party," C.C. said, lowering her voice. "Getting out, seeing people. You know what I mean. He's been acting so totally weird since Elizabeth died."

"No, he hasn't," Meg said quickly.

Meg felt herself blushing because the truth was Dusty *had* been acting weird. Not that he didn't have his reasons. Elizabeth, Dusty's twin sister, had been killed in a tragic gun accident less than six weeks earlier. Elizabeth had stayed at home to work on a history paper while the rest of the family drove to their weekend place at the reservoir. When the family had returned they found her body on the living room floor, a black bullet hole in her temple and her eyes wide open, as if she had been surprised by her own death.

"Did you guys see that ad about Dusty's party?" Roxy Blish ran to catch up with Meg and C.C. She was a pretty girl with pale blue eyes and cornsilk-blond hair. She was so fair that she looked as if she'd been dipped in bleach. No one at school had ever noticed her until she made cheerleader six

weeks earlier. Roxy often thought, with some bit-
terness, that she would have been the perfect spy
because people stared right through her as if she
weren't there. She had done all the same things
Elizabeth Ellis had done—baton twirling in the
seventh grade, tumbling in the eighth, and then
cheerleading and running for class office—but
none of her activities led to anything. Roxy had
begun to feel as if "runner-up" were a permanent
part of her name. Elizabeth had constantly been at
the center of an admiring crowd, and nobody even
knew Roxy's name. Until Elizabeth died, that is,
and Roxy got to replace her on the cheerleading
squad. She was first runner-up.

Roxy looked at C.C. and Meg a bit uncertainly.
"At least I guess it's a party."

"Sure it is. And am I ready for one!" cried C.C.
"I've been hoping somebody would get a party
together. When's it going to be, Meg?"

"Tomorrow night. Saturday. Dusty wants to have
it at his parents' place at the reservoir. It's supposed to last all night and into Sunday."

"Aw right! Neat!"

"My mother and father would never let me go to
a party where there are no chaperons," said Roxy.

"Good grief. Just don't tell them," said C.C.
"What's the big deal? Do you tell your parents
everything? Will you look at you guys? Look at
your faces? You act like you're going to a funeral. I
mean, come on! We're talking about having fun
here. Remember fun? It's what you have on the
weekend. What's the problem?"

4

"I'd better run," Meg said. "I've got to go by my locker."

C.C. watched Meg's red head bobbing away from them through the crowd of kids in the hallway. "I wonder what's bugging *her?*"

Roxy didn't hear. She was lost in her own worries. She hadn't been able to come right out and say why the party invitation made her uneasy, but the truth was she had been avoiding Dusty. She couldn't pretend that she was sorry Elizabeth was dead. She wasn't sorry. She was glad, and she had the feeling Dusty knew.

"Hey, Jeff!" Bryan Whitfield ran to catch up with Jeff Holloman at Jeff's locker. "Did you see Dusty's ad in the paper?"

"Looks like he's having a party."

"Yeah, what do you think? Are you going?"

Jeff hesitated a fraction of a second. "Sure."

"To tell you the truth, I was kind of surprised to see I'm invited." Bryan was a skinny boy who moved with quick, jerky motions. A half-head shorter than Jeff, he had a young, wide-eyed expression that made him seem perpetually startled. He tapped the folded paper against Jeff's locker. "Since Elizabeth got killed Dusty hasn't said two words to me."

"It's been rough for him."

"I know! I know! It hasn't exactly been a picnic for me either, you know. But Dusty's gone off the deep end, I'm telling you. He's getting very strange."

Jeff turned his broad back on Bryan and twirled his combination lock. "So, don't go if you don't want to."

"No, no, no, I'm going! I think we owe it to him." Bryan threw a punch into the air. "I mean, if he's trying to get himself back to normal, we all ought to be there. Help out. You know?"

Jeff hoisted his book bag over one shoulder and slammed his locker shut. "Guess I'll see you at the party, then."

"Guess so."

After Jeff walked away Bryan remained there a moment, sucking air through his teeth. An isolated house out by the reservoir was a funny place for a small party, he thought. It was different if you were going to have a big blast, with people crammed in and lots of noise. You'd need a place out in the country so the neighbors wouldn't call the police. But with just a few kids, what was the point of driving out so far? Dusty must be up to something.

"Bry!" Kristin Jenkins's sharp squeal cut through the hall noise. He blinked, and there she was with her bouncy, shiny brown hair and big blue eyes. "Did you see that funny ad in the paper? Mandy Baumgartner showed it to me. You and me are invited, aren't we?"

Bryan nodded mutely.

"I'm going to a party at Dusty Ellis's!" Kristin gave a sharp little squeal. "I can't believe it. Back when I was an eighth grader I thought you both were gods or something. Big ninth graders!" She giggled. "I remember one time Dusty came into class to deliver a note, and we all just sat there with our mouths falling open, he was *so* neat! And now he's asking me to his *party,* and you and me are going *together.* It's so incredibly neat. It's like what I've always dreamed about, like Cinderella or something. What do you think people are going to wear? I want to look right."

It was kind of sweet the way everything impressed Kristin, thought Bryan. She had had a crush on him for years, it turned out, and he had never noticed. He had been floored when she showed him the little shrine she had made to him in her room. There was a candle and everything, with all kinds of pictures of him—offtakes from the annual, yellowed clippings from the newspaper. "You're all I ever wanted, Bry," she had said, "and now you're mine, all mine." It was a little weird, maybe, almost an obsession, but he enjoyed somebody being intense about him after Elizabeth.

He wondered now why he hadn't broken up with Elizabeth long ago. She had liked pointing out his faults and making him feel insecure. She thought he should stand up to his father, for instance. But he couldn't. She had no idea what it was like living with his dad.

"Just ask what the other girls are going to wear," whimpered Kristin. "Will you do that, Bry? Will you? If I know what they're wearing, then I won't worry."

Bryan wished clothes were all he had to think

about. All he could think about was Elizabeth. Dead. Her brains blown out. But he had to stop remembering that. It was a downer. Kristin was his girlfriend now, and having her around made him feel important. He needed that confidence. Something told him he was going to be able to use it at this party of Dusty's.

2

"You aren't going to do anything stupid, are you, Dusty?" Meg begged, standing by her locker after school.

He wouldn't meet her eyes. "I don't know what you're talking about, Meg. All I'm trying to do is have a party. You don't have to make such a big deal of it." He flicked his blond hair back out of his face with a swift shake of his head. The sun had burned platinum streaks in his hair, and from a distance he looked like the average bimbo surfer. It was only up close that it was possible to see the set, bitter line of his mouth.

"Of course," Meg said, "if you really want to have a party, that's great. I'm just surprised, that's all."

"You suppose all I ever think about is Elizabeth's death?"

"Well, no—"

"I think about it a lot. I admit it."

"That's okay," she said hastily. "That's perfectly natural."

"It's not just natural, Meg. It's *useful*. I've come up with some good ideas. How about this—she was murdered." He stood there, challenging her.

"But it was an accident, Dusty. The police said so."

"The police don't know everything. A couple days ago I picked a floppy disk up off the desk—I thought it was a blank, but it turned out Elizabeth had already written something on it. And you know what it was? Her history paper! Don't you get it? She told us she had to stay home to work on her history paper, but she'd already written it! Meg, she'd already written it!"

"But all that tells you is she wrote the paper before—well, before it happened," Meg finished lamely. "She might have written it on Saturday after you left."

"Nah. The police said she died sometime Saturday." Dusty shook his hair out of his eyes. "She didn't write the whole thing on Saturday. You know how she always put things off. . . ." He blinked away tears.

She hesitated. "I'm lost. I'm not following you."

"Listen. She had to have already written the paper, but it doesn't make sense that she'd done it beforehand unless she had other plans for the weekend that she didn't want to tell us about. Like what if she had fixed it up to meet Bryan at the house while we were gone?"

"But Bryan was campaigning in Raleigh with his parents! He wasn't even in town." Bryan's dad, who had been a state senator for years, was now running for governor of North Carolina.

"I'm not saying I've got all the answers. There's a lot I don't know. Like what was Elizabeth doing with the gun out in the first place? She wouldn't just take out a gun and stroll into the living room with it for no reason. It doesn't make sense. Also, when I think about the way the room looked when we found her—it was fixed up like a stage set." His eyes were cold and unfocused, and he seemed to be staring through Meg to some horror only he could see.

Meg could not bring herself to point out what everyone thought had happened—that Elizabeth had committed suicide.

Dusty's eyes focused and bored into her as if he had read her mind. "And if you think she did it on purpose, you can forget it"

"I d-didn't say—"

"You think I don't know what people are saying?" he said bitterly. "Well, they've got it all wrong. Why would Elizabeth kill herself? Everything was fine. Besides, she wasn't the type to give up. You know how she always thought she could fix everything. She never went around being depressed."

"There's something to what you're saying," Meg admitted. In Meg's opinion, Elizabeth's problem was that she thought she could fix other people's lives. That was the only explanation Meg could come up with for her pairing off with a wimp like Bryan. "You really think she was murdered?"

Meg told herself it was good she and Dusty were talking. For weeks she had been afraid even to mention Elizabeth's name to him. It was better to get things out in the open. And, she thought, there *was* sense in what he said. If suicide was ruled out, Elizabeth's death was mysterious.

"I can think of only one reason for her having that gun." Dusty's eyes narrowed. "Somebody threatened her. Maybe there was a struggle for the gun."

"But there weren't any signs of burglary, were there?"

"It wouldn't have to be a burglar who did it. There were people right in school who wanted Elizabeth dead."

"Oh, no, Dusty!"

"Sure there are. That ditz Kristin is one of them. You think she's sorry that she finally has a clear field with Bryan? One day in the cafeteria I heard her say, 'I'd *kill* for a date with Bryan Whitfield.' It's not something you forget. The past few days I've been asking around about her. It turns out Kristin has a really weird thing for Bryan. The funny thing is I happen to know Elizabeth used to see her in peer counseling." He laughed mirthlessly. "Little did she know that all the time she was counseling Kristin, Kristin was sticking pins in a voodoo doll with Elizabeth's name on it. I'm not making this up! Turns out you can get voodoo dolls at the flea market out on Highway Three-oh-one.

Some Haitian immigrant is doing a booming business. I went out there myself to take a look."

"Who told you this stuff, Dusty?"

"Michelle Overby, for one. Turns out Kristin bought a so-called love potion and asked Michelle to put it on Bryan's salad at lunch. Michelle thought it was hilarious."

"Did Michelle do it?"

"Heck, no. Not everybody's as dumb as Kristin. This is a girl who has—I have this on good authority—a shrine to Bryan in her room and who actually burns a candle to him there."

Meg's mouth fell open.

"I know. I could hardly believe it either. Of course, everybody who knew about it thought it was funny. But suppose it wasn't just funny. Suppose it was crazy. The kind of crazy that would make Kristin kill Elizabeth."

"I can't believe it."

"Well, take your pick. What about Roxy Blish? She didn't even pretend to shed a tear when Elizabeth died. Roxy never could compete with Elizabeth, and now she doesn't have to. She was runner-up for cheerleader, now she's on the squad. Six weeks ago nobody had ever heard of her. Now she's in hog heaven, our Roxy." He added bitterly, "And she's practically living in Jeff's pocket. She's stolen my best friend on top of everything."

"I'm sure Roxy's sorry about Elizabeth, Dusty. Anybody would be."

He laughed. "You think everybody feels what they're supposed to feel? Well, it doesn't work that way. And pretending everything is okay isn't going to catch Elizabeth's murderer. I'm going to have to bend some rules to do that."

"What do you have in mind?" Meg asked anxiously. "What exactly is going to happen at this party?"

"We're going to play a game, Meg. A game to catch a murderer." His face was expressionless. "I just hope I've invited everybody. Elizabeth had this friend she used to go shopping with sometimes—Hilary was her name. I always thought there was something funny about her."

"You must have the name wrong, Dusty. There isn't anybody we know named Hilary."

"I think she went to South Parker or something. Black hair. Wore too much makeup and weird clothes. I only saw the girl a few times, but she looked like a real loser to me."

"Maybe Elizabeth was trying to help her. You know how she liked to help people."

He shrugged. "Maybe. But why wasn't this Hilary person at the funeral? I looked for her, and she wasn't there."

"Dusty, you can't honestly think Elizabeth was murdered by some girl who went shopping with her a few times!" Meg regarded him uneasily, wondering if he was losing his grip on reality.

"No, of course not." He shook his hair back. "Anyway, I've got to go ahead with the people I've got."

C.C. suddenly appeared beside them, and Meg glanced at her. How much had C.C. overheard?

"Can I bring a date to the party, Dusty?" asked C.C.

"Sure."

C.C. smiled and scooted away before Meg could speak.

"Why did you tell her she could bring a date?" demanded Meg. "You know that she's only going to bring that horrible tennis pro from the club."

"Jeez, Meg, listen to you. What does it *matter?*" He frowned suddenly. "I got to go. I got a lot of things to take care of to get ready for the party." He smiled thinly. "Nobody's at home to help me out."

Meg winced as he strode away. She knew that Dusty's life had been turned upside down the day they found Elizabeth's body. His mom had collapsed and was now recovering in a sanatorium somewhere in Florida. Since that had happened, his dad had found one excuse after another to be out of town on business, as if he couldn't face the emptiness of the house. Dusty had lots of reasons to be bitter. It was no wonder he had changed since Elizabeth died.

He used to be so much fun, and such a nice guy. Meg remembered when he had rescued her kitten from a tree and had slid down, gently cradling the frightened little bit of fluff, not even noticing that his face was scratched and bleeding. That was the Dusty she had fallen for. He never teased or ganged up on people the way the other boys did. When he came charging into the dimly lit corridors of the school, the place lit up for Meg. He had a characteristic way of banging his locker shut with a sharp suddenness that she could identify from far down the hall. She'd know when he had arrived, and her heart would beat quickly. Minutes later he'd slide into the desk next to hers in homeroom, dump his books on his desk, catch her eye, and grin. Jeff, likely as not, would crack some joke then and ruin their mood. Jeff's clowning got on Meg's nerves. But she understood that when you went with Dusty, you got his best friend, too. It was like a package deal. And it was natural because Meg knew Dusty had never spent much time alone. Not since he and Elizabeth had shared a double stroller and a secret language. He was all extrovert.

Lately he was different, though. He stared blankly through people as if they weren't there. If Jeff cracked a joke, he didn't get it, or at least he didn't laugh. He looked, Meg thought, as if he'd just been pulled out of a car after a terrible automobile accident.

Of course, she had expected him to be knocked out by Elizabeth's death, but she figured it would be better in a few weeks when he got over the initial shock. Actually, it *had* gotten a little better. At least he was eating lunch again instead of just picking at it. He was talking. But there was no way she could pretend he was back to normal.

A party to trap a murderer? The whole idea made Meg nervous, and she had a momentary impulse to cut and run. After all, no law said she had to go to Dusty's party. She could say she had a headache or something. Sometimes she wondered if he would even miss her, he seemed so out of it. Once or twice he gazed at her with such empty eyes that she had the wild thought that Elizabeth was speaking to him from the grave.

She unfolded the newspaper C.C. had handed her during the algebra exam with Dusty's ad circled in blue. "You're invited to a murder . . . It'll be a blast!" I'm being silly about this, Meg told herself. It's just a party, after all. What can possibly go wrong?

By that same evening all of the guests for Dusty's party had concocted innocent-sounding excuses to give their parents for where they'd be Saturday night.

For C.C. it took no effort at all. Her mother and father had long since quit noticing what she did. The year before, C.C.'s sister Monica had fallen apart at college and started hearing voices. One morning she had wandered into the school's ornamental fountain stark naked, and the Carmodys had gotten an emergency phone call from the school. Ever since, they had been completely focused on Monica's treatment, Monica's medication, Monica's hospitalization, Monica's halfway house, Monica's refusal to take her medication, Monica's repeat hospitalization, until the very sound of her sister's name set C.C.'s teeth on edge. Sometimes she felt as if she'd scream. Not that anyone at home would have noticed. They were too busy worrying about their elder daughter to notice anything about the younger one. C.C. felt she was constantly turning the volume of her life up, but that nothing she did could begin to compete with Monica's spectacular craziness. She had tried coming in drunk, had filled the bathroom with cigarette smoke, had let her grades slip, and had taken up with a thirty-year-old boyfriend, but her parents barely noticed. She wondered what she'd have to do to make them realize they had another daughter. It would have to be something incredibly desperate, something unbelievably destructive.

"I think I'll spend Saturday night with a friend," C.C. said.

"Mmm. Okay. Sure." Mrs. Carmody was reading a new book with a purple and white cover—*Living with the Chronically Mentally Ill.*

"I'm not sure when I'll get home," C.C. added.

Her mother didn't even look up.

"Dusty and me are going out to the reservoir Saturday," Jeff told his mother that night. "We'll probably spend the night out there."

Mrs. Holloman touched Jeff's arm and smiled. "Darling, that's wonderful!"

"It's no big deal. Maybe we'll get in some fishing."

"You haven't seen much of Dusty lately, have you?" She hesitated. "I mean, I couldn't help but notice."

"He's been awful down, Mom."

"That's when friends really need us, Jeff. Maybe Dusty's not much fun right now, but it's not a time to think of yourself."

"I'm not!" yelped Jeff. "Jeez, I mean, there's not much I can do when he as much as tells me to buzz off."

"Just be there for him."

Jeff ran his fingers through his curly dark hair. It wasn't as easy as his mother thought. He couldn't force himself on Dusty.

"Well, anyway," his mother went on more cheerfully, "this fishing trip of yours is the first step in the right direction. He may be ready to open up."

Jeff was within an inch of telling his mother about the unchaperoned party, but he knew it would be a mistake. She would have been sure Dusty was up to no good. That was the way her mind worked. His dad's, too. If you could believe Jeff's parents, the world was a bunch of crimes waiting to happen. It probably came from his dad's being a cop. And the worst part was that Jeff was afraid he was starting to think the same way. He had a real bad feeling about this party. The day before Dusty had been a recluse, nursing his grief twenty-four hours a day, and now he was a wild party animal? It didn't make sense.

Not that Jeff claimed to know what was going on in Dusty's mind. They had practically quit speaking. It was grim. Jeff just hoped the party was a sign Dusty was getting back to normal.

The last thing he wanted was for his mom to keep asking him a bunch of questions about him and

Dusty, so he got in his car and headed over to see Roxy. She had become a big part of his life lately, he reflected, stepping on the gas. She wasn't a part of his usual group, and he had never really noticed her until she got on the cheerleading squad. Then it was as if a light bulb had gone on inside him, and he realized she was the one he wanted.

He remembered the day it had happened. He was at the lunch table with a fifty-cent piece over one eye and his lip tucked up so his front teeth showed, doing his impersonation of Lord Bobo, one of his usual lunchtime characters. "Braw-coli? I say, I never eat broccoli. It's a matter of principle, don't y'know? How could I face all those motherless little broccoli sprouts. Couldn't live with myself, ektually."

Roxy had laughed, and he had glanced over at her table with surprised delight. The fifty-cent-piece monocle fell out of his eye, rolled, and landed against his plate as he bobbed his head in a quick little nod of acknowledgment.

"Don't get conceited," Melissa Anders told him. "That's Roxy Blish, and she's probably laughing at everything today." She lowered her voice and shot an anxious glance toward Dusty's end of the table. "She's going to be replacing Elizabeth on the cheerleading squad. Turns out she was first runner-up in the tryouts last year." Melissa turned around in her chair. "Congratulations, Roxy," she called.

Roxy's eyes were bright with happiness. "Thanks."

All the girls at the table turned to talk to Roxy

then. Jeff, who had older sisters, knew this meant Roxy's status had moved up a notch. She was "in." It was as if she had suddenly become visible.

The next day she had boldly come over and sat at their table, right next to Jeff. She smelled fresh and clean, as if she washed her hair every morning. He studied her for a long time. "Duh, what's up, doc?" he said hoarsely. Never taking his eyes off her, he chomped on a carrot stick.

She grinned. "Are you ever, like, normal?"

"Not if I can help it." He took her hand. "Did I ever tell you I read palms?" He traced the long line of her palm with his finger and felt a shock of warmth go through him. "This line means you and me are going to have a lot of fun together."

"Don't let him get to you." Meg laughed. "He's not certifiable, I promise you."

Roxy took her hand back. "Oh, he doesn't bother me. I've always wanted to be somebody's straight man."

"Is that sort of like being a second banana?" C.C. asked blandly.

Roxy flushed with anger and embarrassment. Jeff knew how she felt. Once or twice he'd wanted to punch C.C. out himself. He met Roxy's gaze with complete sympathy, and all of a sudden—*bong*—he knew he was in love. Now, pulling up in front of the modest frame house where she lived, he felt himself grow warm with pleasure. He got out of the car, leapt over the low cast-iron white fence, and began dodging the lawn decorations. The Blishes had flamingos as well as a pair of cement elves that stood beside a birdbath. But it was the flowers that were the real hazard. There were boxes of pansies, clay pots of chrysanthemums marching up both sides of the steps, and quantities of hanging baskets that were constantly threatening to brain him. Wouldn't that look great in his obit, he thought— brained by a geranium.

The inside of the house was as heavy on decoration as the outside. The Blishes went in for cuckoo clocks, crushed velvet chairs, and shelves of knick-knacks, like porcelain elves hunched under mush-rooms caps and mice with stocking caps. What caught Jeff's attention most were the huge full-color framed pictures of Roxy on one wall. Roxy in a little flip skirt striking a pose with her baton back in the days when her legs were skinny. Roxy in the Little Junior Miss contest back when her legs were pudgy. And Roxy with a ventriloquist's dummy the night she had won the Kiwanis talent competition. Jeff had never figured out if all this stuff was the Blish family's idea of good taste or if it was an immense practical joke. He didn't ask because he had noticed early on that Roxy's family embar-rassed her. Her dad was a round-bellied man with a voice like that of a drill sergeant, and her mother was an intense little woman with tightly curled blond hair who spent all her free time working on church committees. They seemed pretty much like everyone else's parents to Jeff.

Roxy saw him drive up and came out on the porch to meet him. She stood under the porch light, fair and straight like a flame of pure brightness. His heart flipped over. "Let me take you away from all this, my darling," he said as he ran up the steps. "We could live under a bridge, and you could support us both by doing your Robin Leach imitations." Roxy was a gifted mimic, he had discovered to his delight. He thought she was even better than he was. Her takeoff of Mr. Hamnet the history teacher was priceless, but she had to be in a good mood to do it, and a single glance told him she wasn't in a good mood.

"Watch out for the geranium," Roxy warned.

Jeff ducked just in time to avoid possible fatal cranial damage. Then he kissed her, feeling a sudden sweet sadness. He knew that he loved her, and yet it was as if there were a secret part of her that he couldn't understand, as if she were holding something back from him. They sat for a while on the porch swing in the dark, and he kept touching her as if he needed to keep reassuring himself that she was there.

"I've been thinking, Jeff," Roxy began. "I've got a lot of work to do this weekend. I need to get started on that research paper for history, so I think I'll skip Dusty's party."

Jeff stiffened. "You mean not go? Hey, we've got to go. Dusty's—well, he used to be, anyway—my best friend. Got to go to his party."

"You could go without me."

He held her tight. "I don't want to go without you," he said gruffly. "Besides, I'd feel stupid being the only one there without a date." He poked out his lower lip and stuck out his stomach and scratched. "I'd be the poor schmo. Look at Jeff, he's pa-thetic. Poor slob, can't get a date."

She giggled.

"Hey, you aren't worried about your parents, are you? Just tell them you're spending the night with a girlfriend."

"It's just—"

"Don't let me down, Roxy. I *need* you."

By the time he drove away Jeff had gotten Roxy to promise that she would be at Dusty's at the appointed time. She had scared him for a minute. The last thing he needed was to spend the whole party explaining why she hadn't come. The party was going to be awkward enough as it was.

"Of course you can go," Mrs. Whitfield assured her son on Friday afternoon.

"Wait a minute!" Mr. Whitfield objected. "I don't want Bryan staying here alone when we're out of town until Monday." He was an imposing man who looked as if he had been born in a three-piece suit. "I know what happens when parents go out of town. The next thing you know the neighbors are calling the police about some wild party. That's all I need right now," he said, and snorted. "My son getting in the newspapers."

"I'm not having a party. I'm just going over to Dusty's, Dad."

"It's Dusty's first birthday alone without Elizabeth, Henry." Mrs. Whitfield had lowered her voice.

"Oh, all right, I guess you can stay. But for God's

sake take care while we're gone. Don't do anything stupid. I don't want to come back and find that the house has burned down."

"I'm not an idiot, Dad."

Mr. Whitfield's face was suffused with blood. He raised his hand and took a step forward. "Don't you talk that way to me in that tone, young man! I'll knock you clear across the room."

Bryan paled and quickly backed out of his father's reach.

"Don't provoke your father, Bryan," Mrs. Whitfield piped up anxiously. "He didn't mean anything. Did you, Bryan?"

"I'm sorry," whispered Bryan. He could hear Elizabeth's voice inside his head saying, "Your parents talk to you like you're an imbecile, Bry. How can you just sit there and take it?" Easy for her to say. Bryan was embarrassed to admit even to himself how afraid he was of his father. Twice at the emergency room he'd pretended he'd hurt himself falling off his bike, and it seemed as if he'd been wearing long sleeves to hide bruises all his life. But that didn't mean he was a wimp the way Elizabeth had thought. He could sometimes manage to get around his father. He was going to Dusty's party, wasn't he?

Bryan helped his parents load their luggage in the car and respectfully listened to the list of fifty or sixty things he should or shouldn't do while they were gone. Don't leave the toaster plugged in. Don't let strangers in the house. Don't let anybody know you're home alone. Just before they drove off,

Bryan's mother leaned out the car window to kiss him good-bye and whispered, "Maybe you'd better not do any cooking at all, dear. Just the microwave. That should be safe." Her brow was pleated with anxiety. "And be sure to keep everything nice and clean. Please don't do anything to make your father angry, dear. He's under so much pressure lately."

What about me? thought Bryan bitterly. I've been under pressure my whole life. "Yes, ma'am," he murmured.

She patted his cheek, "There's my good boy."

"Elaine, are you going to sit there fussing over the kid all day?" snapped Mr. Whitfield. "Lock your door."

The engine roared, and Mrs. Whitfield's head snapped back as her husband took off. Car engines wore out fast with Mr. Whitfield driving.

Bryan swallowed hard as he watched his parents drive away. He hated his father. His mother tried to pretend that if Bryan would just behave everything would be fine. Bryan always did try to do what his father wanted, but it didn't work. He had the bruises to prove it. He turned and walked back into the house. It was funny to realize that his parents were gone. Really gone. Soon they would be miles away. He felt as if he were coming to the surface after a long time under water. Freedom was fizzing in his blood like champagne.

He jumped into his own car and drove to the Pizza Inn—no having to ask permission. No groveling at his dad's feet. It was great. He'd eat at the Pizza Inn every meal while they were gone. He certainly had no intention of using the microwave the way his mother had told him. As far as he was concerned, the four basic food groups were sweet, salty, crunchy, and slurpy. He could pig out on junk food very happily for days. After he got some pizza, he thought, maybe he'd drive to Raleigh to see the eleven o'clock *Rocky Horror Picture Show*. He hadn't been to Raleigh in weeks—not since Elizabeth died—and he needed an escape valve. He was achingly sick of being the candidate's wholesome son. What was really great was to sit in the *Rocky Horror* audience with a bunch of freaks, nobody knowing who he was, nobody recognizing him. Then he could relax. He decided he'd spend the night in Raleigh in a motel with a pool. Yeah. No danger his parents would find out he wasn't at home. He knew from experience how hectic things got on the campaign trail, and they weren't about to call home late at night when they might wake him up. The city was only an hour's drive away. He could get back from Raleigh the next day in plenty of time for Dusty's party.

4

"Nice location." Rick Eason cast his gaze down along the lawn of Dusty's house toward the country club. From where he stood he had a perfect view of the courts where he slaved every day in the hot sun teaching rich kids like Dusty Ellis to play tennis. "Man, you can practically spit on the tennis courts from here, can't you?" Rick gave C.C.'s waist a squeeze. "Ready to party, sugar?"

"I'm always ready to party."

"Me, too. Just lead me to the beer." Rick smiled, and tiny creases showed at the corners of his eyes. Broken capillaries on his cheeks and nose told of too many cigarettes and too much beer. He was a passably good-looking man with a ready smile, but he looked used up. Unconsciously the others edged away from him a little.

Meg remembered how much Elizabeth had disliked just seeing Rick around the club. She had been convinced he was bad for C.C. "I bet I know a way to get rid of him," she had said to Meg the week before she died. "Just watch." Meg didn't have the remotest idea of what Elizabeth had had in mind, but somehow she felt that if Elizabeth had lived, she would have brought it off. Elizabeth had had a habit of getting her way.

"I thought we'd ride out to the reservoir together in my van," said Dusty. "I've already got the stuff packed. You can leave your cars here."

Meg opened the rear doors of the van and slid in the white box with Dusty's birthday cake inside. She had planned on baking the cake herself, but Dusty had told her it was all taken care of. All she had to do was pick it up at the bakery.

She wished Dusty had been willing to give her some hints about how the murder game was going to work, but he refused to give out any details.

"Should we just get in the van?" Roxy asked.

"Where's Bryan?" Dusty frowned.

"Did he say he was coming for sure?" Jeff asked. "He might have changed his mind."

"Maybe he had to go out of town with his parents after all," said Meg.

"No, he's coming," said Dusty. "He told me. I'll go call his house and see what's holding him up."

Just then a white Toyota pulled up in front of the house, and Bryan leapt out. He was followed by Kristin, struggling with a suitcase and a garment bag.

"Hi, guys!" Bryan slung a duffel bag over his shoulder and trotted over to them.

"Kristin's not just staying overnight. She's emigrating," sneered C.C., eyeing Kristin's luggage.

Bryan threw his duffel bag into the back of the van, then threw Kristin's stuff in on top of it.

"Well, now that everyone's here, we can get going," said Dusty.

As Dusty backed the van out of the driveway Meg twisted around in her seat. "So, Bryan," she asked brightly, "how's your dad's campaign going?"

"Same as always." Bryan shrugged. "Lots of boring banquets and phony smiles."

"Uh, you help him a lot, don't you?" Meg glanced over at Dusty. "I mean, I guess you're pretty indispensable to him, always right there doing what he needs, constantly at his beck and call, huh?"

"Mostly I just show up. Son of the candidate isn't exactly a major role. I just smile and try not to do anything wrong. I'd be at it right now if I wasn't here. Man, if it weren't for your party, Dusty, I'd be sitting on a platform, clapping for Buford Junction's Pumpkin Queen."

It seemed obvious to Meg that Bryan couldn't have gotten away the weekend Elizabeth died without his parents knowing it; she wished Dusty could see it, too. It hit her then that it was going to be pretty awkward with Dusty treating half his guests as murder suspects. Even Miss Manners might wonder what to do to make a party fun under those circumstances.

Meg glanced back at Roxy, who sat rather grimly, with her hands folded in her lap. No, Meg told herself, turning away. Roxy couldn't have committed murder just to be on the cheerleading squad. It was utterly ridiculous. People didn't do that kind of thing. Still, she thought, stealing another look at Roxy, Elizabeth is dead. And there was something so strange about Roxy. Whoever had talked about a "mystery wrapped inside an enigma" might have been trying to describe her. Meg was sure no one could ever guess what was on Roxy's mind. Meg couldn't even remember seeing her at school until she replaced Elizabeth on the squad. She had an amazing ability to fade into the background.

Dusty drove by the Pizza Inn and picked up some pizzas before turning the van south. As they sped along to the reservoir through woods dark with tall pines, conversation languished. Perhaps it was the heat. It was unseasonably warm for October. With the rain coming, Meg figured the heat would break and was glad she had brought a sweater. Dusty steered lazily with one hand. Traffic was light, and the black clouds capping the hot afternoon sky made the woods appear livid and unreal.

"Looks like rain," said Jeff.

"We'll be there before it comes down," said Dusty.

C.C. unbuckled her seat belt and scrambled awkwardly up onto Rick's lap. "Is it my fine tiger-toy?" she cooed.

"Sure thing." Rick laughed and cast a lazy and contemptuous glance around the van. He wondered how much each of these kids was worth. A whole lot, was his guess. They might not have much actual cash on hand, but there was plenty at home. He'd heard them talking around the club about their beach houses, their condominiums and weekend places. He had seen their big houses and fancy cars. There was lots of money here, all right. He just had to figure out how to get hold of it. Light a match under one of these kids' feet and their parents would come up with the cash pretty fast, he bet. Like if you kidnapped one of them, for example. Dopey, helpless little kids. Not one of them with the sense God gave geese. He'd like to see them try to make it out of some of the tight spots he'd been in.

"Hey, are you okay?" Jeff whispered to Roxy.

"Fine." Roxy looked out at the deserted quarry they were passing. Stagnant water filled it, hiding heaven knew what, she thought with a shudder. Maybe old tires and snakes. Soon they were past the quarry, but the image of the quarry and the ugliness hidden under its calm surface lingered in her mind. She wished she hadn't told Jeff she'd come to the party.

At last the trees began to thin, and they became aware of vacation houses here and there. Dirt driveways and mailboxes appeared at intervals along the road. Then the cleared area widened, and they could see the old two-story frame house that had belonged to Dusty's grandparents. It sat beside a reservoir ringed with trees. Only a few houses had been built at this end of the lake, and all of those were closed up for the winter.

Dusty parked the van next to the storage shed behind the house, and Meg scrambled out quickly.

"I think I felt a drop of rain," C.C. cried, jumping down from the van on the other side. "Hurry up. Let's get the stuff inside."

"Give me a hand with the luggage, Jeff." Dusty tossed the house keys to Meg.

She hurried toward the back door, balancing the cake box on one hip. Inside the house was not so hot as she expected. It didn't smell stuffy, either, which was odd. She put the cake down on the counter and peeked around the kitchen a bit anxiously. Quiet and still, the way it was now, the house seemed menacing. There must be a simple explanation for the fresh air. Dusty had told her he had come down to get a few things ready for the party. He might have left a window open. She moved quickly into the living room–dining room area but saw no open windows there. Going into the hall, she passed the stairs and then peered into the single large bedroom on the ground floor. There she was startled to see twisted brown leaves stirring on the braided rug. The crisp brown curls of leaf scudded across the rug, and a fresh breeze touched her cheek. She turned her head and saw that one of the panes of glass in the door to the porch had been neatly removed. Crumbs of glass were still embedded in the putty along the edges. That meant the pane had not shattered but had been deliberately removed. Meg became painfully conscious of the beating of her heart. Someone had broken into the house!

5

Meg turned on her heel, ran back to the kitchen, and threw open the kitchen window. "Dusty!" she yelled, startling the others, who dropped their bags. Realizing she sounded hysterical, she forced herself to calm down. Outside the clouds were so ominously low and dark, it seemed like dusk.

Dusty came running. "What is it? What's wrong?"

"Somebody's broken into the house."

"Jeez, no!" He glanced around. "What'd they take?"

"I don't know. It seemed like something was wrong, so I went around and saw a pane of glass in the downstairs bedroom door is out."

"Maybe it got hit by a branch or something."

When Meg showed Dusty the missing pane in the master bedroom he swore softly and agreed that it had been deliberately removed. The shards of broken glass had been swept up and taken away, almost as if the intruder had been afraid of leaving fingerprints. "We'd better check around to see what's gone."

"Hey, what's wrong?" Bryan stood in the doorway of the room.

"Looks like we've had a burglar. See if they got the television in the living room. C.C. knows the house. She can help. Meg, check out the kitchen."

They split up and checked the entire house. Except for the pane of glass that had been removed, nothing seemed to be missing. Dusty went around the house a second time, double-checking. At last he returned to the kitchen, puzzled. "I don't get it. Nothing's gone."

"Unless it's food they were after," Meg suggested. "We wouldn't necessarily notice if they made off with cheese and crackers."

"Seems like a lot of trouble to go to for cheese and crackers." Dusty threw open the refrigerator. The light came on, displaying an assortment of colas and what looked like a lifetime supply of Mr. Ellis's favorite Canadian beer. "You can't tell me they came looking for food and didn't take the beer."

"Maybe they just wanted a place to sleep." Kristin's eyes were wide. "Maybe they're coming back tonight!"

"Stop it, Kristin," snapped Roxy. "You're giving me the creeps."

"No problem," said Rick. "We just get a piece of plywood or a board and nail it over the missing pane."

"Rick's very handy," said C.C. "He can do any sort of thing around the house."

"Got a hammer, Ellis?"

"Out in the shed. Hang on, I'll get it."

"Hey, Dusty, do we just unpack anywhere?" C.C. asked. "I want to change."

"Let's you and me take the room at the head of the stairs, C.C.," said Meg. "Kristin and Roxy can go in the room next to us, and Jeff and Bryan and Dusty can share the big room across the hall. Uh, Rick, you can put your stuff in the bedroom downstairs."

Rick grinned, and the skin at the corners of his eyes creased. "Want me to be the first one the burglar gets, huh?"

It was simpler than that. Meg knew that nobody would be comfortable rooming with Rick. C.C. might like to pretend that he was just one of the kids, but it wasn't so.

"Nice place," Rick said when Meg showed him the master bedroom. His eyes swept over the white crocheted bedspread stretched on top of blue sheets and the television at the foot of the bed. An open door showed a glimpse of the modern bathroom Dusty's parents had added to the master bedroom. "I noticed this house when C.C. and me came out to the reservoir last summer, but this is the first time I've been inside. Very nice. Elegant."

C.C. noticed Rick already had a can of beer in his

hand. "Don't you want to unpack your things, Rick?"

"In a minute. I might need to help Dusty get the broken pane boarded up first."

C.C. took her bag and headed up the stairs. She was amused at the way Meg had assigned the rooms, keeping the boys and girls as far apart as possible. Meg was always acting like somebody's mother. Well, thought C.C., nobody could make a person stay in her own room.

From the room at the head of the stairs she could hear Dusty hammering a board. Sound bounced around in an old house, and it wasn't easy to tell where it was coming from. C.C. remembered this house had been the perfect place to tell ghost stories when they were kids—lots of frightening creaks and thumps.

When C.C. cracked the window open a bit she could hear the grumbling of the wind in the trees. At once it began rushing in in restless fits and starts, tossing the fringe on the bedspread. She dropped her bag on one of the beds. Rick could be such a royal pain, she thought irritably. If he started drinking the minute they stepped in the house, he was going to end up drunk for sure. Sometimes she got so mad at him, she could— Abruptly she stopped herself with a shiver. Lately she had the feeling she was losing control, and the last thing she wanted was to end up like Monica. She unzipped her bag and began throwing her clothes out of it. The truth was she couldn't really blame Rick for boozing it up. The others acted as if he had a communicable disease. She remembered Elizabeth practically taunting him her last time at the club, acting as if she had something on him. C.C. pushed the thought away uncomfortably. So what? Rick never claimed he was a saint. Anyway, Elizabeth was dead now, and C.C. didn't care what other people thought of Rick. She could go out with anyone she wanted. It was a free country.

A sudden flash of lightning lit up the room, followed in a couple of seconds by the distant rumble of thunder. C.C. threw the window open and stared with longing at the lightning-streaked sky. She loved storms, and this was going to be a crashing good one.

"Did you find the room okay?" Meg's voice floated up the stairs to her.

"Sure," yelled C.C. "Don't worry about me."

Meg went back to the kitchen. Finding that a burglar had been in the house chilled her. An enemy had penetrated the house, but Dusty was acting as if nothing had happened. Dusty had gotten some paper plates out of the pantry and was serving pizza that he heated up in the microwave. Meg glanced uneasily at Rick's beer, wondering how many he had had.

A few raindrops blew against the kitchen windows with a rattle. Meg stretched over the sink to close the window.

"Just leave it up, Meg." Dusty pushed the hair out of his eyes impatiently. "It's stifling in here."

She shrugged. The rain hadn't begun in earnest, but already a damp breeze swept into the kitchen, ruffling the curtains. "It's going to start pretty soon."

"It better not," said Dusty. "Part of the game is outside."

"No problem," said Bryan. "I brought a raincoat."

"And I brought an umbrella," put in Kristin.

"Yeah, but *you* brought *everything*," said Bryan.

Meg switched on the outside light and watched it shine on the short path to the shed and the blue van just beyond. Overhead, trees were bending as if in a gale. The ominous whisper of the wind in high branches filled her with apprehension.

"I hope the lights don't go out," said Kristin.

"It's just a rainstorm, Kristin," said Bryan. "Not a hurricane."

"I guess I'm nervous." Kristin giggled. "I mean, doesn't it give you the creeps to realize that burglars have been in here? What's to stop them from coming back?"

"We've boarded up the window, for one thing," said Dusty.

"Yes, but in these old houses there are so many ways people can get in." Kristin's voice sank to a whisper. "What if they're here now, and we don't even know it?"

"Get a grip, Kristin," snapped Bryan. "We just searched the whole house."

"But not the attic. Or the basement."

"Cut it out. You're going to get us all spooked."

"Eat up, folks." Dusty's eyes shifted. "We want to get moving on the game before it starts to pour."

C.C. came in and pulled a chair up to the table. "I hope you guys saved me some pizza. So where did you get this murder game, Dusty? I hope it's one I've already played so I know the answer."

"You're out of luck, C.C." said Dusty. "I made this one up myself, and it's a little different from the store-bought kind."

"Goodness, that was creative of you," said Kristin. "I'm impressed."

"The problem with the ones you buy," said Jeff, "is they hardly ever have the right number of characters, and sometimes the characters are all girls, and sometimes they're all guys."

"Yeah, that's what I thought," said Dusty off-handedly. "This way I can fit it to who's here. Like I said, it's something a little different. Actually, it's a mystery scavenger hunt."

There was a sudden loud clatter, and everyone jumped.

"It's just the ice maker." Dusty smiled.

Meg got up, filled her glass with ice, and ran water over the cubes. She wasn't hungry at all. What if Kristin was right and some psychopath was hiding in the basement, just like in a creepy movie? "Well, it wouldn't hurt to check the basement and the attic, would it, Dusty?"

"You heard me say we have to get down to the game right away."

"Wait a minute," said C.C. "Dusty, if you made up the scavenger hunt, you can't play."

"Sure, I'll play. I'm the scorekeeper."

"I hope we don't have to go down in the basement," said Kristin. "I think we should all stick together."

"You have to split up. That's the only way it works," said Dusty. "Whoever comes back with the most things on the list wins. When you solve your first clue, come back here, and I'll give you another one."

Kristin's eyes widened in dismay. "You mean we have to go around all by ourselves?"

"Well, in pairs," said Dusty. "The problem is that with me being the scorekeeper, we don't have an even number. Rick, you want to go alone?"

"Sure. More my style anyway." Rick went to the refrigerator and pulled out another beer. Meg wondered if it was her imagination that he seemed unsteady on his feet.

"Okay, everybody finished with the pizza?" Dusty asked a minute later. Without waiting for an answer he began picking up the paper plates smeared with tomato sauce. "Bring on the cake, Meg."

Meg peered into the cake box. As she had feared, the icing had sagged a little from the heat, but what bothered her most was that the cake didn't quite look like a normal birthday cake. It had "Happy Birthday, Dusty" written in icing in the center and seventeen candles, but around the edge were written the words *Eenie, Meenie, Miney, Moe.* Meg shot an anxious glance at Dusty, afraid to ask him what it meant.

She lifted the round layer cake out of the box, lit the candles, and carried it to the table.

Roxy stared at it. "Eenie, meenie, miney, moe? What does that mean?"

"It's part of the game," said Dusty. With the knife he scored lines in the icing, dividing each word in half to show how the cake could be cut into eight fat slices. "The people with matching slices will be partners."

"Piece of cake!" said Jeff. "Yuck, yuck," he laughed.

Everyone groaned. Dusty blew the candles out with a long, powerful puff.

"Ooo," squealed Kristin. "You get your wish. What did you wish, Dusty?"

He smiled. "It's a secret." When Meg met his eyes she was surprised at how cold and empty they were. He didn't even seem to realize he was looking at her. There was a distant rumble of thunder. Meg hugged herself and shivered.

6

Meg watched Dusty give Bryan the other half of the portion of cake marked "Eenie." Bryan was going to be her partner in the scavenger hunt, which was okay. She didn't care who she got paired with as long as it wasn't Rick. That smarmy smirk of his made her flesh creep. She sank her fork into her cake and heard a *clink*. Prodding the cake into crumbs, she pulled out a clear plastic ball, the sort that contains cheap prizes in supermarket vending machines.

"Ooo, look!" cried Kristin. She held up a clear plastic ball between her thumb and forefinger. "I've found a prize!"

"That's your first clue," said Dusty.

Staring down at the round plastic ball on her plate, Meg saw that it had a strip of paper rolled up inside. When she twisted the ball it came apart easily, and the strip of paper fell out. The typed message on it read "Beau shoot. An anagram."

"I guess we aren't supposed to read the clues aloud, are we?" asked Roxy. "After all, with a scavenger hunt the object is to find more of the things on the list than anybody else, so we don't want to give anybody else help, right?"

Meg realized she was staring at Roxy and had to jerk her eyes away. Ever since Dusty had pointed out that Roxy had a motive for killing Elizabeth, Meg wasn't quite comfortable around her. Roxy's pale, expressionless face with its penciled eyebrows and startling pink lipstick gave no clue to her thoughts, and Meg secretly felt she was capable of anything.

"So where's the list of the things we're supposed to look for?" Roxy went on.

"There isn't a master list," said Dusty, "and with this game you won't need one. You'll know what you're looking for once you find it. When you find your first item, come back here, and I'll give you your next clue. But each pair has to put the two clues together first. One partner's clue tells you where to look, and the other tells you what you're looking for."

They pushed their chairs away from the table, and partners began conferring. Meg and Bryan retreated to the pantry near the back door where they could compare their clues in private. "Mine doesn't make a bit of sense. 'You got a bang out of me.' What can that mean?" Bryan unfolded Meg's strip of paper. "Yours is even worse. 'Beau shoot'?" He looked at Meg anxiously. "What does it mean?"

"Well, *beau* is an old-fashioned word for boyfriend. Here, let me see." Meg took her slip of paper back from him and frowned at it. "You didn't finish. Didn't you see that underneath it says 'An anagram'?"

"Yeah, but I don't know what that means."

"It means the letters are scrambled up. 'Beau shoot' is really something else. It's like a word jumble." Meg bit her lip. She'd always been good at word jumbles, but they didn't usually have as many letters in them. This one must be a very long word. Or maybe several words. Then she remembered that Dusty had been anxious to get the game started before it rained, and suddenly it came to her. "Boat house!" she cried. "Our clue must be in the boat house out by the lake! See, if you rearrange the letters in *beau shoot* you can spell *boat house.*"

A gust of wind rattled the back door, and they both jumped violently. "I'm getting my raincoat," said Bryan, swallowing.

"Don't worry about the rain. You aren't going to melt. What we really need is a flashlight." Just then Meg spotted one sitting on top of the fuse box. She grabbed it and flipped it on with her thumb. Luckily, the batteries were still good. "Let's go out through the downstairs bedroom," she said. "It won't be so obvious we're going to the lake as if we went out the living room door."

Bryan decided to run upstairs for his raincoat.

Going through the living room, they passed Roxy and Jeff headed in the other direction, but to Meg's surprise there was no sign of Dusty in the living room. Meg had thought he'd be there ready to give people their second round of clues. Perhaps the first bunch of clues were so tough that he knew he'd have lots of time before anybody was ready for the second set. Meg opened the door to the hall, glanced up the stairs, and saw C.C. and Kristin disappearing upstairs.

When Bryan came back down he and Meg tiptoed down the hall, floorboards creaking under their feet. Meg hated the old house. It seemed to be full of whispers and shadows. Opening the door to Rick's bedroom, she was relieved there was no sign of him. A lamp beside the bed had been turned on, and his suitcase still lay unopened on the bed.

"There's the boarded-up pane in the door." Bryan's voice quavered. "I just hope whoever broke in isn't coming back."

Meg was afraid if she started thinking about burglars she'd be too scared to go outside, so she quickly pushed open the door to the screened-in porch. The old house had originally had a long screened porch that ran across the entire lake side of the house, but the Ellises had had most of it torn down so they'd have a better view of the lake from the living room. Only this bit of porch off the master bedroom remained. Standing at the door and peering out through the screen, Meg could barely make out the dark silhouette of the boat house. She switched on her flashlight and, after a moment's hesitation, stepped out onto the porch. A thump and a rattle sounded directly overhead, making what seemed to be a tremendous noise in the confined space.

"What was that?" cried Bryan.

"I think it was a pine cone landing on the roof." Meg gulped. Dead leaves scratched against the screens with a dry rattle. A few fat raindrops swept in. Meg pushed open the screen door and cautiously stepped off the porch into the darkness. At once the wind sent grit into her eyes and swept her hair across her face. She squinted hard as her eyes filled with tears, and, half blind, she stumbled toward the boat house.

"Want me to get Kristin's umbrella for you?"

"No! Oh, for heaven's sake, Bryan! Come on! We can be there and back by the time you go after the umbrella. We've got to hurry if we expect to win."

Bryan tagged along reluctantly. "Watch out you don't slide," he warned. "It's started raining a little, and the ground's slippery. You could break a leg," he called.

"Oh, come on!" said Meg in exasperation. "Don't be such a scaredy cat."

The boat house loomed before them. Suddenly Meg remembered that the burglars could be hiding in there, and she was glad she wasn't by herself. Bryan might not be much help, but he was better than nothing.

The boat house door creaked as she pushed it open. Tightening her grip on the flashlight, she whispered, "This has to be the place." The air in the boat house had the distinctive smell of mildew, and she could hear the water lapping against the flooring that ran around three sides of the opening, its sound magnified now that they were inside. She was conscious that the Ellises' boat, the *Elizabeth Ann,* was moving a bit on its moorings. The beam of Meg's flashlight spotlighted a coil of rope, then a heap of life jackets.

"Do you think what we're looking for could be in the boat?" asked Bryan.

"I don't think so," said Meg. "It's supposed to be in the boat house, not in the boat. I wonder how we'll know when we've found it."

"Maybe it'll be gift wrapped."

"Very funny." Meg played her flashlight on the pile of life jackets. "Look under those, Bryan. I'll hold the light."

"I hope there aren't any spiders. I hate spiders." Bryan gingerly picked his way past the tangle of rope.

"What was it your clue said?" asked Meg. " 'You got a bang out of me?' Is that right?"

"Yup." Bryan began tossing life jackets aside. Suddenly he stiffened. "My God!" he whispered.

Rick had a pleasant buzz in his ears, and his nose was slightly numb. Not that he was drunk. Just happy. After everyone had left he found one of the clear plastic balls on the floor. Deliberately he ground it into splinters under his heel. A fat lot he cared about Dusty Ellis's stupid game. He wasn't about to go chasing around just because some rich kid told him to. He had other ideas. Big ideas.

He glanced around quickly. When he was sure the others were all out, he went into the hall and tiptoed upstairs.

A bit later he stole back down to the living room. So far, so good, he thought. Now all he needed was a little bit of luck, and he'd be set for life. A smile played across his thin lips as he wandered back to the kitchen, got another beer out of the fridge, and popped it open.

* * *

C.C. felt that having ditsy Kristin as her partner in the scavenger hunt had to be some kind of nasty cosmic joke. She couldn't stand Kristin's chirpy little voice, much less her nerve-shattering squeal. If only she could have switched partners with someone else, she brooded, but everyone else just took off without even bothering to finish eating the cake. The logical move would have been for her to pair off with Rick and let Kristin be on her own, but it was obvious there was no chance of that now. Rick was pretty close to being blitzed, and she doubted he was even going to bother with the scavenger hunt. That left her stuck with Kristin.

"I'm just so glad our clues don't lead to the basement," whispered Kristin.

"How can you be so sure?"

"Mine says 'Ambition will take you there.' That's got to be to the top of the house, right? Maybe even the attic."

"Unless it's on the roof." C.C. took nail clippers out of her pocket and cleaned under her thumbnail.

"I hope it's not out there!" Kristin let out a squeal of dismay. "I am *not* going up on the roof. It's starting to rain, and that roof is two stories high. I'd break my neck."

"I could live with that." C.C. pocketed the clippers.

"Why do you have to be so mean?" Kristin's eyes filled with tears.

C.C. smiled at her. "Dunno. Guess it's just a gift."

"I've never done anything to you."

C.C. sighed. "Kristin, would you cut the complaining and get to the clue?"

"You figure it out, if you're so smart. It's your clue."

"We're a team, now, remember? Besides, my clue doesn't make a bit of sense." C.C. frowned at her strip of paper. " 'You can buy me at the same place you get love potion.' "

Kristin's face reddened, and C.C. studied her with sudden interest. "Is it dirty or something? I didn't catch it." She cocked her head. " 'You can buy me at the same place you get love potion.' I still don't get it. Okay, Kristin, go ahead. I give up. Tell me."

Kristin turned away. "Let's go upstairs."

"Is it something personal?" asked C.C., following her. "Is that why you're turning red, white, and blue all over? Come on, tell me. You can trust me."

"Why don't you just lay off?"

C.C. was beginning to enjoy herself. Maybe this scavenger hunt wouldn't be so bad after all. With any luck, Kristin would be in tears before it was over. "Here's the attic." C.C. glanced up. A string with a tassel on the end hung from a large trapdoor in the ceiling of the hall. C.C. tugged on the string, and slowly the trapdoor came down. A wooden ladder was bolted to the door. It only needed to be unfolded. C.C. pulled it into position. "You want to go up first?"

"No." Kristin drew back. "You go first."

"It's okay for me to turn my back on you, isn't it? You aren't going to stab me or anything?"

Kristin's fists were clenched. "Will you shut up?"

When C.C. got up in the dim attic she saw a bare bulb with a string attached hanging from a beam nearby. She inched over to it, being careful to avoid falling through the open trapdoor. The attic was so full of junk that there was little space for her to maneuver. She pulled the cord and blinked as the bare bulb went on before her eyes. Now she could make out some of the shapes. They were boxes and chairs, bedposts and mattresses shrouded in bedspreads—all ghostly presences.

Kristin's head appeared in the opening. "Have you found it?"

"It'd help if you'd give me a hint about what we're looking for. Is it really a love potion?"

Without answering Kristin climbed up the ladder and stood for a second looking around in confusion. When she tried to move she tripped over a set of folding chairs and had to grab onto an overhead beam to steady herself.

"Better watch your step," said C.C. "I've never seen so much junk in my life."

A scraping, rattling noise on the roof made them both jump. "What was that? Who's there?" shrieked Kristin.

C.C. found that she was breathing unevenly. "I

guess the wind is just blowing branches against the roof."

The old house creaked, and the wind whispered along its eaves as they stood frozen in the pool of yellow light cast by the bare bulb.

Kristin shivered. "I'm really glad there's a light up here, at least."

"Only about twenty-five watts," C.C. grumbled with a sudden shiver. "I don't see how we're supposed to find anything. It's hardly bigger than a Christmas tree bulb."

"That's going to make it simple!" cried Kristin. "Don't you see? Whatever it is, it's bound to be under the light. Otherwise, Dusty would know we'd never find it."

"You know, I think you may have something there." C.C. opened her eyes wide in surprise.

"I'm not as stupid as you think."

"I knew you couldn't be," retorted C.C. She cautiously felt her way among the boxes heaped near the light, a trickle of sweat sliding down her back. It was stiflingly hot in the attic, though she could hear the wind outside nibbling at the edges of the house with a high-pitched whine. The pale shrouds over the furniture moved unnervingly. It was the wind coming in under the eaves that made them flare out, C.C. told herself, but her heart thumped painfully. "This must be it," she cried. She lifted up a package wrapped in silver foil with gold ribbon. It glimmered under the light of the bare bulb.

"Are we supposed to open it?"

"Sure! What else?" C.C. tore the package open and flung the paper and ribbon aside. Inside was a white cardboard box full of excelsior. "Must be something real little." When C.C. groped in the excelsior her fingers felt something smooth, almost oily to the touch, like a candle. She fished it out and stared at it, puzzled. It was a crude wax doll with a pin through its heart. It had blue beads for eyes, and affixed atop its crude head was a brunette doll's wig several sizes too large. It was as if the maker had stripped the wig off a long-haired doll and then given it a short straight haircut.

"No!" gasped Kristin.

"What's going on?" C.C. stared at her.

Kristin's fingers pressed hard against her cheeks. "Don't you see? That doll is supposed to look like me!"

Suddenly everything went black.

"The light's blown." C.C. tried to make her voice calm. "Don't move, Kristin. We don't want to fall through the trapdoor opening." The utter blackness was like a complete blotting out of sensation. If it hadn't been for the nagging of the wind, C.C. might have imagined herself in a grave. Slowly an uncomfortable thought rose in her mind—it was darker than it should have been. Why wasn't light coming from the trapdoor opening? They should have been getting some light from the hall. "It's not just the attic lights that are out." C.C.'s voice was uncharacteristically jerky. "The house lights must be out, too." Suddenly she heard a thump and a muffled oath below. Then the trapdoor was shoved up and slammed shut with a bang.

"We're trapped," shrieked Kristin. Her sudden scream split the silence.

8

"I'm glad you're with me, Jeff," Roxy said nervously. "I would hate to go down in the basement by myself."

"Boo!" Jeff grabbed her around the waist.

Roxy pushed his hands away. "That's not funny! You scared me."

"Do you know what you get if you put three blondes ear to ear?" Jeff grinned. "A wind tunnel."

"Now, that's *really* not funny."

"Oh, come on, Roxy. It's nothing personal. It's only a joke."

She bit her lip. "I know I'm jumpy. I can't help it. This isn't like any scavenger hunt I've ever heard about."

"That's because Dusty made it up. He's good at that kind of thing. Last year at Elizabeth's and his birthday party they made fortune cookies for everybody. Dusty wrote all the fortunes." Jeff grinned. "I remember mine said, 'You will be the Great Fruit of the Loom.'"

"It's never going to win the Pulitzer Prize. Let me see your clue again." She frowned at it. "'The baseball team that has the worst season ends up here.' It's got to be the cellar. Okay, here goes."

Jeff pushed the door to the basement open and flicked on the light switch just inside the door. Roxy closed the door behind them. She didn't want the others to know they had almost solved their first clue. Her heart was pounding so hard she felt Jeff could hear it. She had always been a little afraid of the dark. Particularly when it was accompanied by a dank smell. She firmly pushed her fears down. C.C.'s crack about her being a second banana had really made her mad, and she wanted to put in a respectable showing on the scavenger hunt to show the others she was as good as they were. "What we're looking for must be down here somewhere." She inched down the bare wooden steps into the shadowy depths of the basement.

When Jeff reached the concrete floor he kicked over an empty cardboard box. He couldn't see much except bare pipes along the ceiling, more cardboard boxes, and the hulking black furnace. He was wondering what to do when the light suddenly went out.

The darkness seemed to press against Roxy, suffocating her. It was strangely disorienting. She turned her head first one way and then another, unwilling to believe there was no hint of light anywhere. But all was black, and her heart fluttered fearfully.

"Don't move, Roxy," said Jeff. "The bulb must have blown. If you trip over something, you might hurt yourself."

"If only I had left the door open," moaned Roxy. "I just didn't want anybody to see where we'd gone. Who would ever think the stupid light would go out? Oh, stupid, stupid, *stupid!*"

"I'm going to try to get over to the steps," said Jeff. "Keep talking so I can tell where you are. That'll help me navigate."

"Jeff! Did you hear that?"

"What?"

"It sounds like somebody screaming."

"You must be imagining it. I can't hear anything. Ouch." Jeff rubbed his forehead. He had banged his head against something and couldn't figure out how it had happened. He should be coming up to the steps, he thought, but everything seemed to be in the wrong place. Panic swept over him. Be calm, he told himself. Breathe deep. Sooner or later he'd find the steps. He had to. He couldn't keep going around in circles indefinitely.

"Are you okay, Jeff?" Roxy asked anxiously. "Say something."

"I sure wish I had a pack of matches right now."

"Or even a key chain that glows in the dark! What if nobody knows where we are? What if they just find our bleached skeletons years from now?"

"You aren't helping any, Roxy. Hey, I think I've found the steps."

"Be careful!" she cried. "Don't try to walk up them."

"Don't be stupid. How can we get out of here if I don't walk up them?"

"What if you fall? Oh, don't do it, Jeff. We can just wait here for somebody to come after us."

"Don't worry, I'm going to be real careful. I'm going to feel my way."

Roxy could hear faint scraping sounds as Jeff made slow progress up the steps. The darkness seemed to weigh on her chest, making it hard for her to breathe. It wasn't like the darkness in her bedroom at home, where chinks of light came in around the blinds and under the door. This darkness was unnatural, as deep and featureless as if they were inside the belly of a monster. She wasn't sure she could stand it and felt she might begin to gibber nonsense. "I can't hear the screaming anymore," she said faintly.

"Maybe whoever was doing it died," Jeff growled. When he reached out he felt the cold smoothness of the cellar door and groped for the knob. He felt that if he didn't get out of the cellar and see some light soon, he would go stark raving nuts. Suddenly the light came back on as mysteriously as it had gone out. "Well, I'll be darned." Jeff threw the door open, grinning widely in his relief. "Next time let's prop the door open while we look."

"Forget any next time!" said Roxy, running up

the steps behind him. "Nothing could get me to go down in that basement again." At the top of the stairs, stopping to catch her breath, she darted a glance toward the kitchen. She felt dizzy, almost physically sick with relief.

"I wonder where the others have gone," said Jeff.

"I wish we could just go home. This place gives me the creeps, Jeff. I don't want to spend the night here." It occurred to her that she was going to cry, and, choking, she turned away.

"Hang on, Roxy." Jeff's hand rested on her shoulder and gave it a comforting squeeze. She glanced around at him and was surprised to see that he, too, appeared to be visibly shaken. Something about the house was threatening, she thought, licking her dry lips. As if the house could read her mind and condemn her. She reminded herself that the house couldn't possibly know her secrets. But an uneasiness crept through the old place, with the wind.

Jeff pulled the drawers open in the kitchen one after another, just in case Dusty had put his keys there. No such luck. Breathing unsteadily, he ran his fingers over the top of the microwave, then lifted up one cookbook after another, letting each fall with a plop. The keys! Where could they be? He wanted to borrow Dusty's van just long enough to drive Roxy home. He was beginning to regret that he had pressured her into coming. Something funny was going on. Why else should the lights go out like that?

Roxy peered anxiously out the kitchen window. "It's starting to come down really hard now." A crack of thunder shook the window panes, and suddenly the rain was pounding and spattering the ground outside.

Rick poked his head into the kitchen and leered at them. "Do you know where they keep the pretzels, man?"

"Aren't you even going to mention the lights going out?" Roxy asked sharply. "Did you even notice? We were trapped down in the basement for practically hours."

Rick shrugged. "They came on again, didn't they? What are you complaining about?" He collected a bag of pretzels from the pantry and went back into the living room. Roxy decided that the only reason Rick wasn't scared was that he was too drunk to know what was going on. Roxy felt a momentary impulse to pick up one of the half-eaten slices of cake and smash it against Rick's face. That would wipe the smirk off.

"Somebody just tried to kill us!" wailed Kristin. She burst into the room with C.C. close behind her.

Rick popped a pretzel in his mouth. "Oh, come off it! Why would anybody want to kill you? Don't be stupid."

C.C. collapsed into a plump armchair. "Honestly, Kristin, the lights went out, that's all. Pull yourself together. It was no big deal."

"Somebody had us trapped up there," gasped Kristin. "It's not my imagination, you guys. I heard the trap door bang shut as soon as the lights went out. And look at this!" She waved the wax doll as if it were a trophy.

"Hey, it looks sort of like you." Rick snickered. "It's got the same eyes, same haircut."

"See!" squealed Kristin. "I told you, C.C.! It does look like me! Dusty's trying to kill me!"

"What is that?" asked Roxy.

"Some kind of voodoo doll," said C.C.

"Oh, yuck!"

Jeff put his arms around Roxy and gently stroked her hair. "Voodoo, hoodoo," he sang in her ear. "Hoodoo you love, yeah!"

"You see how that pin is stuck right through her? Right through the heart?" Kristin lowered her voice dramatically. "That means I could have a heart attack."

"Or else acid indigestion." Jeff grinned.

"I don't know how you can joke." Roxy shuddered. "I've got the absolute creeps. We were stuck down in the basement when the lights went out," she explained to the others, "and it really was creepy."

A spatter of rain swept the windows, and they all turned violently.

"Where's Bryan?" cried Kristin. "Oh, what if something awful has happened to him?"

"I just wish I knew where Dusty was," said Jeff.

In the long silence that followed his words the rain beat hard against the house. They were huddled together in the living room like some frightened primitive tribe around a campfire at night,

Roxy thought. She was morbidly conscious of the rainy darkness that engulfed them. Voodoo didn't seem silly at all to her right at that moment. She had the eerie sensation that the old house was listening, waiting for some catastrophe to befall them. She bit hard on her trembling lower lip.

"I figure Dusty's hiding someplace, pulling the strings to make us dance." Rick's words jumped out of the silence like an alarm.

"What do you mean by that?" yelped Kristin.

Rick shrugged. "All I know is what I hear, folks. Dusty's been acting weird. That's what C.C. tells me."

"Do you think he's—dangerous?" Kristin's voice shook.

"No!" The word seemed to be torn from Jeff. "Dusty wouldn't hurt us." He shot a quick glance at Roxy.

"Not if he's in his right mind," said C.C. slowly.

"Of course he's in his right mind." Jeff was becoming uncomfortable.

"I guess. But he's said one or two things that have made me wonder," said C.C. "Like I think he's got it in for Bryan."

"Maybe Bry is dead already!" wailed Kristin. "And Dusty's coming after us next!"

Jeff found Roxy's hand and held it so tightly that she pulled it back, wincing. Roxy wondered what Jeff was thinking. He knew Dusty better than anyone. Was Dusty capable of taking some bizarre revenge for Elizabeth's death? Her skin crawled at the thought.

"Don't be stupid, Kristin," said Jeff steadily. "Dusty wouldn't hurt Bryan."

"Okay, but where is he?" asked C.C. "I'd feel a lot better if Bryan and Meg were here. It's true that Dusty has been acting weird. He never hangs around with us anymore, does he? And I've seen him stare at Bryan like he hated him. Another thing"—C.C. glanced around at the others—"does anybody think the lights went out just now by accident?"

Rick laughed abruptly and wiped the back of his hand across his mouth.

"I can't stand this anymore," cried Kristin. "I don't care if my folks ground me for the rest of my life! I'm going to call my dad and tell him to come get me!"

"Go ahead. There's the phone." But when C.C. turned around it was gone. Only the bare phone jack showed that a phone had once been plugged in beside the couch.

Roxy was miserable. What could they do? They were stuck in this isolated old house with no way to leave. She felt so exposed. If only there were some safe place to hide! But Dusty knew the house better than anyone. He'd find her wherever she hid.

Kristin's fists pressed against her cheeks. "This is it," she shrieked. "Now we really are trapped!"

9

The darkness in the boat house seemed to close in around Meg when she heard Bryan gasp.

"No!" Bryan repeated weakly.

Meg's hand was shaking, but she steadied her flashlight as best she could on Bryan's back.

"What is it?" she cried. "What's there?"

"It's a gun!"

Meg pushed past Bryan and continued to shine the flashlight on the heap of dusty life jackets. A dull glow of metal winked up from their midst. Bending over, Meg saw that the gun lay surrounded by old life jackets. It was a big, no-nonsense-looking automatic.

"What can a gun be doing here?" Meg whispered.

"Dusty left it here!"

Meg fished her clue out of her pocket, stepped back a bit, and shone her flashlight full on it. "You got a big bang out of me," it read. She scowled.

"That's a funny way to put it, isn't it? It ought to say 'You can get a big bang out of me' or 'I make a big bang'—something like that." Then she remembered that Dusty suspected Bryan of murdering Elizabeth, and she fell silent. The clue sounded like an accusation, she realized, because it *was* an accusation.

Bryan was so stiff it was as if he had been stuffed. His eyes were round and bulging, and in the harsh light of the flashlight he was bleached deathly pale. "It's the gun that killed Elizabeth!" he whispered. "Dusty thinks I shot her." Suddenly he keeled over. Meg stared, astonished at him lying limply on top of the gun. "B-Bryan?" For one horrible instant she thought he was dead, but when she knelt beside him she saw that he was breathing.

A noise came from the direction of the boat. Meg leapt up suddenly, and the flashlight fell to the floor with a clatter and flickered off. She stood very still, straining her ears, but all she could hear was the drumming of a few raindrops on the roof of the boat house. She held her breath, suddenly aware of the profound darkness. She couldn't see anything, neither Bryan nor the boat. Damp air blew in from the open doorway, but the square of dim light she expected to see wasn't there. The light from the house must be out, she realized, shivering. What could that mean? She inched backward slowly and jumped when she heard another scraping sound and then a bump. Someone else was in the boat house! With a quick intake of breath she pressed herself against the wall.

Near the boat a beam of light bobbed, and Meg stared at it in fascination. The light was moving toward her! Someone was coming after her! She shrank back against the rough boards of the wall as the flashlight beam searched the boat house, shining first on the rough boards of the wall and then on the pile of rope.

"Meg?" said Dusty's voice. "Are you okay?"

Her knees almost gave way with relief. "Dusty! You scared me to death."

"Where's Bryan?"

"He's right here. He passed out or something. I think we're going to have to call a doctor."

The beam of Dusty's flashlight found Bryan's Reeboks and his skinny ankles and then quickly played over his jeans and shirt. Bryan stirred. "He killed Elizabeth," said Dusty in a strange voice. "That's why he fainted when he saw the gun. Well, now we know."

"He fainted because he was scared," retorted Meg. "It's amazing I haven't fainted myself."

Bryan groaned. He seemed to be trying to push himself up.

"He's coming to," said Dusty. "I'd better get out of here. I don't want him to see me. If anybody asks, you don't know where I am."

"Dusty, what—"

"You're the only one I can count on, Meg." Dusty switched off his light. "Remember—not a word."

"Give me your flashlight!" yelped Meg.

Dusty handed it to her and then slipped away.

"I can't see!" cried Bryan. "Everything's black. I'm blind! I can't see!"

"Calm down," said Meg. "It's just dark, that's all." She fumbled with the switch of the unfamiliar flashlight and at last got it to come on. It beamed bravely into the darkness of the boat house. "Stay where you are. Don't move an inch, Bry. You're right on top of the gun."

In a panic Bryan leapt up and slammed smack into Meg. The next thing she knew they were a mess of tangled limbs on the floor. The flashlight rolled on the floor and came to rest with its beam illuminating the uneven boards. Meg was so relieved it hadn't broken that for a second she couldn't think of anything else. "Bryan!" Meg cried. "Move. Your elbow is grinding into my stomach."

"Sorry." He shifted so his entire weight seemed to rest on her diaphragm, and for a second Meg was afraid she couldn't breathe. Finally he did manage to scramble off her.

"Watch it!" said Meg. "We're not that far from the edge. You could fall in the water if you aren't careful." When at last she struggled to her feet she realized she ached all over. Why did Bryan have to panic like that? she thought irritably. She picked up the flashlight with a silent prayer of thanks that it was still working. "We'd better get back to the house. I'm worried. The lights are out."

"Maybe we should just stay here awhile," said Bryan.

"You don't have to go if you don't want to," Meg said. "I'll go by myself."

"You aren't going to leave me here alone!"

"Come with me, then."

"Hey, look!"

Meg turned around to face the doorway. It was pouring now, and the sound of the rain on the roof was almost deafening. Through the almost solid sheets of water she could just make out a faint glow from the direction of the house. The lights were back on. "I guess the storm must have knocked the lights out for a minute," she said doubtfully.

"We'd better not leave the gun here," said Bryan.

"Why not?" Meg shivered. "I don't want to touch it."

"I'll get it, then."

"Be careful, Bryan. It may have a hair trigger."

"As if you know anything about guns."

Meg sighed. "Well, if you want to take it in, then get it and let's go. But point it at the ground, for heaven's sake."

"It's raining awfully hard."

"It might come down like this all night. Do you really want to sleep out here?" Without another word Meg stepped outside into the storm. The rain immediately plastered her hair to her head, and the downpour was so heavy she could scarcely see. Squinting her eyes half closed, she doggedly slogged toward the light. Bryan had this effect on her, she realized as she pushed her hair out of her eyes. He dithered so much she found herself plunging ahead purely out of annoyance. She was dimly aware that he was following her, but she was past caring. Where was Dusty? What was he up to? If he was trying to scare everybody into fits and then see who broke down and confessed, she didn't think much of his plan. Bryan had gotten scared enough to pass out, but what did that prove? Nothing. He hadn't confessed to anything, either. And if any of Dusty's other suspects broke down and confessed, he wouldn't even know about it. They were inside the house while he was crouching out in the boat house spying on Bryan.

Just before Meg reached the door she stepped into a large puddle. "Great," she muttered. The rain streamed off the roof of the house like a waterfall and directly onto her head. She pushed the door open and stepped, dripping, into the living room.

C.C., Kristin, and Jeff stared at her with open mouths. "Meg!" they cried.

"Where's Bryan?" squeaked Kristin.

"He's right behind me."

"I thought maybe Dusty had murdered him," whimpered Kristin.

"Where did you get such a crazy idea?" Meg wrung her hair out with both hands. Her shoes were soaked to the insoles, and her underwear was sticking to her. What she needed, she thought, was a good hot bath and dry clothes.

"He's trying to drive us nuts with this game," said Kristin hoarsely.

"Don't be stupid!" Meg frowned. "He is not."

"Everybody keeps saying 'Don't be stupid, Kristin.' But it's not me that's ignoring what's right in front of her eyes. It's not me that thinks everything's hunky-dory when we're being stalked by a maniac." Kristin tiptoed over to the window, parted the curtains, and peered out at the pouring rain. "He's probably out there right now, waiting for his chance."

"Do you know where Dusty is, Meg?" asked C.C.

Meg shrugged uncomfortably. She wished Dusty hadn't asked her to say she hadn't seen him.

Bryan came in, his raincoat dripping water on the floor. His eyelashes were so wet they stuck together in spiky clumps.

Rick laughed. "You look like a drowned rat, Bryan. You ought to go take a hot shower right this minute. If you're not careful, you're going to get pneumonia."

"Bry!" Kristin threw herself into his arms.

"Hey, hey. Watch out, there, babe. I'm soaking wet."

"You're alive! Oh, Bry, I thought I was never going to see you again! It's been so awful! We were up in the attic, and somebody locked us in and turned the lights out."

"The trapdoor wasn't exactly locked," C.C. muttered.

"And Dusty made this voodoo doll that looks like me and stuck a pin in its heart. Now I'm a dead duck." Kristin's face was screwed up in a look of woe as she handed the doll to Bryan.

"I don't think you have anything to worry about," said Jeff heartily. "I betcha all those voodoo dolls are U.S. Grade A inspected and safe for all ages. Hey, this is the U.S.A., folks. Not Haiti.

When was the last time you knew anybody who died of a hex, huh?"

"Well, somebody did steal the phone." Roxy's voice was tense.

Rick steadied himself against the couch and smiled at her goofily. "Have you thought that maybe it isn't Dusty doing all this stuff?" he said.

"Who else could it be?" C.C. looked blank.

Rick shrugged. "Somebody else was in the house, remember. Those burglars. They could have Dusty tied up somewhere."

Meg swallowed hard. Why had Dusty set up his party way out in the middle of nowhere? Kristin was right—it was creepy. She wished she had demanded to know exactly what Dusty was up to. She was almost as much in the dark as everybody else. Even if Dusty only meant to find Elizabeth's supposed murderer, she had the uneasy feeling that things were spinning out of control. No one had counted on burglars breaking into the house. What if this was their hideout? They could be lurking in the house or any of the outbuildings.

"Wait a minute," said Roxy. "It doesn't make sense for the burglars to gift-wrap a voodoo doll and leave it in the attic. The only person who could have done that was Dusty."

"Dusty probably doesn't realize how much this little game of his is getting to everybody," said Jeff.

Bryan awkwardly fished the gun out of his rain-coat pocket. It was so large it stuck a little in the lining, and he had to twist it to get it out. Kristin gasped, and Jeff stepped in front of Roxy protectively.

"Put that gun away, Bryan," said Meg. "Put it on the kitchen table."

"What did you think, Jeff?" Bryan smiled. "That I was going to shoot Roxy?"

Jeff took the gun from Bryan and turned it over carefully, then handed it back to him. "Looks to me like you've got Mr. Ellis's SIG-Sauer PTwo-twenty-eight."

"You mean this is the gun that killed Elizabeth?" cried Meg. "How can you tell?"

Jeff cleared his throat. "Well, it's got Dusty's dad's initials on it, for one thing. Mr. E. showed it to me last year when he bought it. I was interested because the police department was talking about getting some of them."

"I'll go put it on the kitchen table." Bryan shed his raincoat, hung it on the coat rack by the pantry, and took the gun into the kitchen.

Meg darted an anxious glance at the kitchen door as it swung shut behind Bryan. "I can't believe the police gave the gun back to the Ellises."

"Why not? Elizabeth's death was an accident, wasn't it?" Jeff flung the phrase at Meg.

"Dusty doesn't think so," she said. "I guess that's why he put the gun out in the boat house for Bryan and me to find."

"I don't get it," said Jeff. "What's he trying to prove?"

"Dusty's gone 'round the bend," said C.C. "I

think we ought to lock all the doors and figure out how to get help."

"Why bother to lock the doors? The house is like a sieve," cried Kristin. "All these doors. All these windows! All Dusty has to do is heave a brick through one of them and climb in."

"Don't be an idiot." Meg said. "Dusty may have gone a bit overboard with this game, but he's not a maniac."

"How can you be sure?" Kristin whispered.

"I just know." Meg had to admit she was feeling a little uneasy herself when she remembered the odd sensation she had had lately that Elizabeth might be speaking to Dusty from the grave. It was impossible, of course. That was something that only happened in ghost stories. But the idea that the thought even crossed her mind showed how strange Dusty had become lately.

"I think we ought to search the house," said C.C.

"C.C., you can't think that Dusty is nuts!" Meg said.

"I don't think anything, Meg. I just wonder where he is. I say we look for him."

"Makes sense to me," Jeff put in. "After all, he could be lying somewhere hurt or something. Heck, he could have broken an ankle when the lights went out. Let's split up and comb the house."

"I don't want to be all alone anywhere in this creepy house," cried Kristin. "Go with me, Bryan."

Meg reluctantly agreed to join in the search. She wondered if there was any chance they'd actually find Dusty. Most likely, he was still hiding out in the boat house.

"Let's check the upstairs bedrooms, Meg," said C.C.

"Wait for me, Bry!" squealed Kristin, following him toward the kitchen.

"I'll take the basement," said Jeff. "Roxy, you take a look in Rick's room."

Rick continued to sit slumped on the couch. They all knew he wouldn't budge to help them.

Jeff didn't want to make a big deal of getting to search the basement alone, but he had gotten very curious about what he and Roxy were supposed to find down there. This time he carefully left the door ajar. Once downstairs he systematically began turning over the cardboard boxes that littered the floor. It didn't take him long to find what Dusty had left for him—a package neatly wrapped in gold foil and tied with gold twine. He held it a second, reluctant to open it. Come on, he told himself. How bad can it be? He tore the wrapping paper off, pulling out handfuls of excelsior, and a small doll fell to the concrete. He picked it up. It was the sort of old-fashioned Kewpie doll that had been given as a prize at county fairs. It was made of the cheapest plastic and wasn't in very good condition. Someone had painted a black dot in the middle of the doll's forehead. Painted on the doll's bib in rough letters was the single word *Liz*. His lips pressed together, Jeff carefully tucked everything— doll, excelsior, and wrapping paper—back under the box where they couldn't be seen. Then he straightened up and stood there for a minute, staring ahead sightlessly. What could this mean? Had Dusty really gone around the bend, the way C.C. said?

When he emerged from the basement C.C. was waiting for him. "I guess he wasn't down there, huh?"

Jeff shook his head. "No such luck. I'll go outside now and check the van," he said. When he opened the back door he hesitated a moment, then turned up his shirt collar and plunged out into the rain.

A minute later, soaked to the skin, he was banging on the door to the van. The floodlights from the house shed too feeble a light to be any help, and the rain made a terrific racket that drowned out everything else. The doors were locked, and he couldn't tell if anybody was in the van or not. He jogged around to the back of the van and tried the back door. To his relief, the handle twisted in his hand. He jerked the door open and crawled inside. It felt so great to be out of the rain he was tempted to prolong the search, but it was instantly evident that Dusty wasn't hiding in the van. After all, a guy Dusty's size wouldn't exactly fit in the glove compartment. After a minute he climbed out of the van and ran back to the house. Roxy was waiting for him in the kitchen. "Any luck?"

He shook his head.

"We didn't find anything either, so we finally gave up. Meg was going to take a shower, but Rick said Bryan should go first because he was in worse shape. It turns out he fainted when they found the gun."

"No kidding! He actually fainted?"

"Is he epileptic or something, Jeff?"

"Nah, just a scaredy-cat."

"I don't feel so brave myself." Roxy's voice quavered. "After the others came back downstairs I went up and went through all of Dusty's stuff, hoping I'd find the keys to the van. I didn't. You know what that means. We're stuck here no matter what happens. What if—"

"What if what? You've got to calm down, Roxy. You're shaking like a leaf," Jeff said, and he wrapped his arms around her.

"I have this feeling Dusty is stalking me. He's just waiting for a chance to kill me."

"Why would he want to kill you, for Pete's sake?"

She blinked. "No reason at all."

"You're getting as paranoid as Kristin. Look, don't worry. If worse comes to worse, tomorrow I'll go out on the road and flag down a car."

"Nobody's coming out to the reservoir at this time of year." She wiped away a tear and struggled to smile. "I guess I am coming a little unglued. I know it's stupid. You better go upstairs and dry off."

They were halfway up the stairs when the screaming began.

10

Jeff pushed Roxy out of the way and ran ahead.

"What is it?" C.C. was standing in the hall, bewildered. "Who screamed?" People came out of their bedrooms into the hall.

Bryan staggered out of the bathroom. His hair was matted, and he left an ominous trail of red drops behind him.

Jeff could hear Roxy's quick intake of breath behind him.

"Oh, my God," said C.C. "It's his head."

"I can't stand it," Kristin whispered.

"Sit down, Bry," Meg said hurriedly. "Take it easy. I know some first aid."

"I don't need to sit down!" Bryan licked the red off his fingers and giggled.

"It's the shock," said Meg hastily. "I'll get some blankets. Just sit down, Bry."

"It's only ketchup, you idiots!" cried Bryan.

"Ketchup?" Kristin repeated.

There was a long silence as they gazed at one another uneasily.

"I personally do not think this is very funny, Bryan," said Meg stiffly. "We're all on edge, and—"

"Do you think I did this to myself? Don't make me laugh." Bryan stripped off his shirt and clumsily wiped his face. "When I pushed open the bathroom door something fell on my head. All of a sudden I was dripping with this stuff." His eyes widened. "But that wasn't the worst part. A voice kept whispering, 'I know what you did. I know what you did.' I slipped and fell down then and thought I was done for. All of a sudden the voice stopped."

Jeff shuffled uncomfortably. "Now Bry, we're all under a lot of strain—"

"I'm not hearing things!" yelled Bryan. "Listen for yourself!" He hurried down to the end of the hall and pushed the bathroom door open. They gathered around the door, and sure enough Meg heard someone whispering softly, "I know what you did, and I just might tell. I know what you did."

While they froze, mesmerized by the voice, Jeff strode into the bathroom and turned on the light. Meg strained her ears, but the whisperer had stopped. A second later Jeff came out holding a tape recorder. "Here's our voice," he said. He turned the recorder on its back, and the voice began again. But when he flipped the recorder over the voice stopped. He moved his hand in front of the tape recorder. "I know what you did—" the recorder began. Jeff laid the machine on the floor face up, and again the whispering stopped abruptly.

"Weird," said Roxy.

Bryan swallowed. "Of course, I figured it had to be something like that. I mean, it's not like I believe in ghosts."

"It must be fixed up with some kind of electric eye setup, the kind of thing they use to trip cameras in wildlife photography," said Jeff. "It was on the bathroom shelf right by the door. When Bryan opened the door that must have broken the beam and turned it on."

"This is obviously some sort of sadistic game Dusty is playing." Roxy sounded on the verge of hysteria. "I, for one, don't plan to wander around the house waiting for something more to happen. Look at the mess we're in—we can't call for help, we don't know where Dusty is hiding, and we can't leave here. We're totally helpless—like sitting ducks. I'm going to lock myself in my bedroom."

"I guess that makes sense." Jeff watched her run into her room and slam the door. He shook his head. "All this stuff is getting to me, too, to tell you the truth."

"You don't think it's all kind of funny—in a Halloween sort of way?" asked Rick.

Jeff was jolted by the sound of Rick's voice. He hadn't heard the tennis pro come up the stairs.

"It's getting close to Halloween, isn't it?" Rick added with an air of innocence.

"Maybe you wouldn't think it was so funny if it had happened to you," said Kristin.

Rick jabbed Bryan in the ribs. "No problem, unless a person's got a guilty conscience, huh, Bryan?"

"Oh, get lost, Rick." Bryan drew away.

"Pret-ty sensitive, aren't we?"

"Cut it out, Rick," said C.C. "Bryan's had enough tonight."

"I don't think it's one bit funny, turning out the lights like that." Kristin gulped. "And that ketchup all over Bryan. If you ask me, Dusty is sick, sick, sick."

"The lights could have gone out by themselves," suggested Jeff. "Dusty might not have had anything to do with that. It could be just the storm."

"Sure," said C.C. scornfully. "Like we really believe that."

"Well, have fun, kiddies." Rick gave them a crooked smile. "And don't do anything I wouldn't do." He shuffled back down the stairs, whistling tunelessly.

"Roxy has the right idea," said Jeff after a moment. "There's nothing else we can do tonight. Let's all turn in. I just wish I knew where Dusty was. I hope he's okay."

"I'm going to shove my chest of drawers up against the door in our room," said Kristin. "Not that I'll be able to sleep a wink as long as a maniac is stalking us."

"Dusty's not a maniac," protested Meg. No one

bothered to argue with her. They drifted away to their rooms, leaving her alone in the hall. She realized then how uncomfortably damp and sticky she was. While they searched the house for Dusty she had changed her clothes, but by now her wet hair had dripped onto her fresh shirt, her ankles itched, and she longed to wash the gritty mud off her feet. She stood indecisively, wondering if she dared take a shower. After a moment she peeked into the bathroom and switched on the light. The tiled floor was spattered with watery ketchup. A few drops of ketchup even peppered the wall. She pulled back the shower curtain and, with some hesitation, turned on the tap. Hot water poured out of the spigot. As far as she could see, there were no more hidden booby traps. Maybe she'd go ahead and shower after all.

When Meg went back to the room to get her shower things C.C. peered up at her from behind her lurid paperback. "Come on. You aren't going to shower?"

"I thought I might."

"I just hope the bathtub doesn't explode on you."

"I checked it out. It seems to be okay." Meg rummaged in her luggage for her hair dryer. "C.C., do you think Rick could have turned out the lights? All he'd have to do is step into the pantry and flip the circuit breakers."

"Why would he do that?"

"Pure meanness?" suggested Meg.

"You've got some nerve!" said C.C. hotly. "Rick's not the one who dragged us out here to the middle of nowhere to play this creepy game. Rick may not be any hero, but at least he's still in his right mind, unlike some people I could name."

"I'm sick of your snide remarks." Meg flushed. "Dusty's been through a lot lately, and the least we can do is stand by him and not go around saying he's crazy."

"Yeah, but if he talks crazy and acts crazy, what are we supposed to think?"

"You've just got crazy on the brain, C.C., because of what happened to Monica. It's not Dusty who's getting to you. It's your sister."

Meg ducked, and the paperback ricocheted off the wall behind her.

"Get out of here!" C.C.'s face was white with rage. "Get out before I kill you."

Meg darted out the door and shut it behind her. Hugging her shower bag to her chest, she scurried to the bathroom, her breathing coming in fast pants. She never should have brought C.C.'s sister into it, she thought remorsefully. When she locked the bathroom door behind her and tried to catch her breath she felt thoroughly ashamed of herself. She wished C.C. would let her apologize, but she knew C.C. was more likely to lock the room and refuse to listen. Meg had never seen her so angry.

Meg stepped into the shower and turned on the shower full force. She bent her head and let the rush of hot water beat down on her tension-knotted back, then she sudsed up her hair, squeezed her eyes closed, and let the soapy water run over her face. Her worst problem, she realized, was that she was sick with worry about Dusty. If only she knew where he was. He had been hiding in the boat when she and Bryan were out at the boat house, but surely he wouldn't spend the night out there. If he was trying to make Bryan crack up, he'd want to be in the house where he could watch. She didn't see how he could suspect a scaredy-cat like Bryan of murder. Now, if it had been Roxy . . . Meg's soapy washcloth hesitated a moment as a thought took hold of her. Roxy seemed so jumpy. Almost as if she had something to hide. What if Roxy had been Elizabeth's mysterious shopping friend? She had heard Jeff say that Roxy could do a hilarious imitation of Mr. Hamnet. And hadn't she once won a ventriloquist contest, too? Meg remembered Jeff's saying there was a picture of her with her dummy in her living room. Chances were Roxy could change her voice to sound completely different. Put her in flashy clothes with too much make-up and different-colored hair, and she wouldn't be recognizable. It wasn't as if anybody had had a very clear idea of what she looked like before Elizabeth had died anyway. None of them had known her before she replaced Elizabeth on the cheerleading squad. Meg scrubbed her back absently, wondering. It was the kind of joke Elizabeth might get a kick out of—dressing Roxy up and going out with her, nobody recognizing her. But how would they have gotten to know each other? Meg would have sworn Elizabeth hadn't known Roxy either. Was it possible she knew Roxy from peer counseling, the same way she knew Kristin? Suddenly Meg realized there was probably a lot about Elizabeth's life that Dusty didn't know. It wasn't as if they were close the way they had been when they were toddlers. Even twins had their own lives when they got older and had boyfriends and girlfriends. It hadn't seemed worth thinking about until now. But if Roxy was in the habit of coming and going at Elizabeth's house while in a disguise, it certainly would have been a perfect setup for murder. She would have known that even if someone saw her go to the house on the fatal day, there would have been nothing to link a brunette with overdone makeup to the startlingly fair Roxy Blish.

When Meg got out of the shower she felt better. At least she was clean, she told herself. And it was possible that she had an interesting idea to put to Dusty. If he would just show up. In her rush from the bedroom she had forgotten to bring her night-gown and bathrobe, but it didn't matter. She had already decided it would be better to sleep in her jeans. That way she'd be ready to face up to any unpleasant surprises that might hit in the middle of the night.

Meg peeked cautiously out into the hall. There wasn't a sign of anyone. Only the distant rumble of thunder punctuated the spooky stillness. She glanced uneasily at the closed doors up and down the hall and wished someone else were around. It looked as if everyone had gone to bed. The floorboards creaked under her feet as she walked toward her room. Her hand was on the doorknob when she heard a shot ring out.

11

Meg swiftly peered up and down the hall. None of the doors flew open. No one else seemed to have heard anything. Yet the shot had sounded so loud —as if it were right downstairs!

Seized by an overwhelming fear she couldn't define, Meg dropped her shower bag and bolted. On the staircase she almost collided with Bryan. "Watch out!" he said. "You almost ran me down."

"Bryan!" she cried. "You're okay! You're okay! Oh, thank goodness."

"Of course I'm okay. What did you think?"

"I don't know." She gulped. "I guess I just panicked. Didn't you hear it?"

"Hear what?"

"That noise?"

He looked uneasily behind him. "Actually, I did

hear something. I think it came from the kitchen. Sounded like a gunshot."

"Yes! That's just what it sounded like! We ought to make sure nobody's hurt."

"Look, whoever's down there has got a gun." He saw that she was staring at his shaking hands, and he shoved them in his pockets.

"That's okay, Bry," she said kindly. "You go to bed. I'll check downstairs."

"You don't have to be sarcastic."

"I'm not being sarcastic. You don't have to come with me, but I think one of us had better check it out. I-I'll do it." Meg started down the stairs, and after a moment Bryan reluctantly followed her.

Meg's heart was in her throat as she pushed open the swinging door to the kitchen, wanting to shrink back from what she might find. To her relief, there was no dead body on the vinyl floor of the kitchen.

"False alarm," said Bryan promptly. "I guess we can go on up to bed now."

"Wait! Somebody's been in here. The gun's been moved. Didn't you leave it on the kitchen table?" The gun lay near the sink, beside a pair of rubber kitchen gloves, the dirty paper plates from dinner stacked nearby "You must have seen somebody come in here, Bryan. Where were you when you heard the shot?"

He blushed. "In the downstairs john, actually."

C.C. stuck her head in the kitchen. "Has anybody seen Rick? He told me he had a headache, and I've been looking for aspirin for ages. Finally Kristin found some for me, and now he's disappeared."

"He must have gone to bed," said Bryan.

"You're kidding me! I have half a mind to wake him up," said C.C. "The least he could do is hang around and wait for the stupid aspirin after I went to all that trouble."

"Hush!" said Meg suddenly. "Did you hear that?"

"What?" asked Bryan. "I didn't hear anything."

"I did." Meg pushed the door open in time to see Kristin tiptoeing into the living room in a quilted bathrobe.

"Didn't anybody hear me?" asked Kristin plaintively. "I was calling you all."

"I guess not." Meg realized now that she had expected to find a body downstairs. She knew she should feel relieved, but somehow she didn't. It was as if something horrible were still waiting to happen.

Kristin plopped down on the living room couch. "I went to your room to talk, but neither of you was there. Then I heard people rushing downstairs. I was afraid maybe something was wrong and you all had forgotten about me." She pouted. "It's too scary rattling around in this big house. I think we ought to spread our blankets out on the floor and sleep in one room. It's the only thing that makes sense."

Suddenly the front door rattled loudly, and Kristin fell silent. They stared at the door, mesmerized. "Someone's out there," whispered Kristin. "Golly, I'm glad it's locked."

All Meg could think of was "Little pig, little pig, let me come in." She was afraid she might start to giggle hysterically any minute.

"Who is it?" called C.C. shakily.

"It's me, for Pete's sake. Open up." The muffled voice was Dusty's.

C.C. opened the door, letting in a gust of damp air as Dusty squeezed past her. "Let me in! It's pouring outside. I've got water dripping down my neck."

"Dusty!" cried Meg. "Where have you been? We looked everywhere for you."

"I went down to check on the boat. That's all."

"You've been checking on the boat all this time?" asked C.C.

"Well"—he ran his fingers through his wet hair—"I, uh, sort of took a walk, too."

"Sure, you did," said C.C. sarcastically. "In the pouring rain you took a walk."

Roxy came in. "I heard a shot after Kristin left," she said. "A gunshot." She looked forlorn in her shabby green chenille bathrobe. "I tried to come down sooner, but I had an awful time finding my contact lens case."

Meg darted a suspicious glance at her. How long could it take somebody to find a contact lens case? "I thought I heard something, too," said Meg. "But now I'm starting to wonder if it was a car back-firing. Are you positive what you heard was a shot?"

"I have very good hearing," said Roxy.

C.C. ran down the hall and banged on Rick's bedroom door, followed by Meg. "Rick? Rick? Are you in there?" She tried the door and, finding it unlocked, threw it open.

Peering anxiously over C.C.'s shoulder, Meg could see that the room was empty. The bedside lamp shone on Rick's overnight bag, which lay on the bed untouched, still plump and fully packed. The door to the bathroom was ajar. C.C. tiptoed across the room and cautiously peeked into it, as if she expected to find Rick's body facedown in the tub.

While C.C. checked the bathroom Meg checked out on the porch. Rain poured noisily off the roof, and the air was turning chilly. She could see no one in the porch's shadows and hastily stepped back inside.

"Where's Jeff?" cried Meg suddenly. "Why didn't he come downstairs with the rest of us?" Roxy's face seemed to take on the tint of her green bathrobe. She wheeled around suddenly and ran for the stairs.

Alarmed, they all scrambled after her. She pounded on the door, and when no one answered she burst into the boys' room with everyone right behind her. Jeff sat up in bed and regarded them groggily. "Wha'?"

"Didn't you hear me knocking?" demanded Roxy. She flicked on the light.

Jeff blinked and drew the sheet up over his bare chest. "I'm a heavy sleeper. What's going on?" He regarded them in puzzlement. "Good grief, Dusty, you're soaking wet. Where have you been? We looked everywhere for you!"

Dusty mumbled something about checking the boat.

"We can't find Rick now," cried C.C. "He's not in his room."

Jeff shrugged. "So he went out."

"We thought we heard a gunshot," said Meg.

"But it might have been a car backfiring," put in Bryan.

"You know, it probably was a car backfiring," said Kristin. "Anyway, I don't see why everybody's so worried about Rick. He's the one person who can take care of himself."

"You all were plenty keen to search the house and turn it upside down when Dusty was missing," C.C. said hotly.

"Well, we know Rick can't be up here because we've just been in all the bedrooms," Roxy pointed out. "He has to be downstairs somewhere."

C.C. frowned. "Maybe he's drunk and doesn't know what he's doing. Or maybe he's sick. He did say he had a headache. I think we ought to look outside for him."

"Bryan's got a raincoat," said Kristin. "And you can borrow my umbrella, if you want, Bry."

"If you think I'm going out there by myself, you're crazy."

"Give me the raincoat, then," said C.C. "Where is it?"

"On the—the coat rack downstairs by the pantry," Bryan stuttered. "But I don't see why we have to make such a big deal out of this. You're overreacting."

"Anything might have happened to him!" said C.C. "If all the rest of you want to stand around here, go ahead. I'm going to look for him." C.C. stomped downstairs.

A long roll of thunder made them all jump. Then they stood in silence, no one wanting to speak.

Meg was torn between relief and alarm. How marvelous it would be, she thought, if Rick had murdered Elizabeth and become unnerved by the murder game so that he'd made a run for it. It was such a wonderful solution that she hated to examine it too closely for fear it wouldn't hold up. When she recalled Rick's smirking face she had to admit that he had seemed more smug than alarmed. She didn't know what to think. Anything seemed possible as they stood listening to the rain.

Roxy cleared her throat. "We could look in the pantry. He could be in there. Or even in the basement."

"If we're going to search the house again," said Bryan, "I think we ought to stick together. For all we know, he could be lying in wait for us. Maybe he fired the gun just to get us to come out of our rooms. Maybe now he's waiting for us to split up so he can jump one of us."

Meg became alarmed. His theory seemed likely to her. "I think he might have turned out the lights. He wasn't very interested in the scavenger hunt, so what was he hanging around downstairs for, if he wasn't just waiting to turn out the lights?"

"That's easy. He never gets too far from the refrigerator," said Roxy. "It's where the beer is."

Dusty was toweling his hair dry. "Would you guys mind getting out of here so I can get on some dry clothes?"

They stepped out into the hallway, and a moment later Dusty came out, buttoning up his shirt. C.C. ran back up the stairs. "I can't find the raincoat, Bryan."

"That's impossible. I put it right there on the coat rack."

When they all went downstairs to check, there was no sign of the raincoat. Only small puddles of water beneath the coat rack showed where it had been.

"That settles it," said Dusty. "Rick took the raincoat and ran away. That's got to tell us something."

"But what?" asked Roxy.

Jeff came in, having obviously thrown on his clothes hastily. "Okay, will somebody tell me what's going on?"

"Rick stole Bryan's raincoat and then took off," said Dusty.

"I wonder if he took the van." Jeff peered out the kitchen window. "Hey, wait a minute. Come here, Dusty."

"What is it?" cried C.C., pushing up to the window. She uttered a dreadful, animal sort of whimper that rose in an unsteady crescendo to a scream.

12

Though Jeff kept insisting that the girls should stay inside, there was no stopping them from crowding out the door. Ignoring the rain that blew in their eyes, they all gathered around Rick's body where it lay facedown in the mud. The floodlights over the back door shed enough light so that Meg could see that Rick's fingers had clawed furrows in the soft dirt and that hollows in the mud were now filling up with water. Then she saw the black hole in the back of the pale raincoat and rocked back on her heels, feeling sick to her stomach.

Jeff gently laid his fingers at the side of Rick's neck. Meg knew he was touching the carotid artery, checking for signs of life. She hoped she wasn't going to throw up.

"He's dead," Jeff said.

"No!" screamed C.C. "He can't be."

Meg put her arm over C.C.'s shoulder, but C.C.

shook her off. "Get your dirty hands off me! I guess you're all happy now, aren't you? This is just what you wanted."

"You don't know what you're saying, C.C.," Meg said.

"I know exactly what I'm saying."

"Come on, let's go inside," said Meg.

"Are you crazy? We can't leave him out here in the rain!"

"I'm sorry. We can't move him, C.C." Jeff shook his head. "We've got to call the police."

"My dad is going to kill me." Bryan looked sick. "Why did something like this have to happen?"

Kristin whimpered. "I want to go home."

"Where's the phone, Dusty?" asked Jeff.

"I hid it under the sofa."

"I think we'd better get C.C. inside." Meg pushed the wet hair out of her eyes.

"He's dead!" screamed C.C. "How can you just stand there?"

"Come on inside." Jeff pulled C.C. to her feet. "We've got to call the police."

Meg was so frightened she couldn't speak. She remembered the time she had gotten stopped for going fifty-five in a forty-five-mile-per-hour zone. The police officer had stood there like Fate in sunglasses. She had been scared then, but this was worse—much worse. Her mouth was dry and her hands were clammy as everyone crowded back into the kitchen. She could hear Jeff in the living room phoning the police.

Meg opened the refrigerator, looking for something to drink, and was startled to see that only a few lonely colas and a jar of mustard were inside. Could Rick actually have drunk all those beers? If the bullet hadn't killed him, she thought grimly, the beer would have. She decided against a cola and closed the refrigerator door hastily, licking her dry lips.

Dusty gathered up the clear plastic balls that had been hidden in the birthday cake and began putting them down the garbage disposal. They went down with such a racket it sounded as if the disposal was coming apart.

"What are you doing that for?" asked Meg.

"I don't want the cops to get any funny ideas."

"Dusty's right," said Bryan. "I think we better just soft-pedal the whole murder game angle."

"Where's the voodoo doll, Bryan?" asked Dusty.

To Meg's surprise, Bryan produced the small wax doll, and Dusty shoved it down the garbage disposal, too.

"What are you doing?" whimpered Kristin. "Don't you see this means I could end up going down a garbage disposal?"

"Don't be silly," said Bryan. "You wouldn't fit down a garbage disposal."

Jeff came in. "The police are on their way. I called my dad, too."

"Where's that Kewpie doll, Jeff?" Dusty asked urgently. "The one from the basement."

"Dusty's put the voodoo doll down the garbage disposal!" wailed Kristin. "I'm under a serious curse."

"Wait a minute, Dusty," said Jeff. "I don't think we'd better destroy evidence."

"Do you think I killed Rick?" demanded Dusty.

"No. No, of course not."

"Then none of this stuff is evidence, is it? It'll just confuse the cops."

"I don't care," Jeff said stubbornly. "I think we'd better leave everything just the way it is. It's going to look worse if we try to clean things up."

"Did I hear someone say something about the basement?" Roxy's eyes flicked anxiously from Jeff's face to Dusty's.

Neither boy paid any attention. "So you aren't going to tell me where it is?" Dusty glared at Jeff.

"Nope. I'm not."

"Some kind of friend you are."

"May I call my dad now?" whimpered Kristin.

For Meg, the time after they telephoned their parents was the strangest of all. An enormous silence hung over them as they privately struggled with their fears. Meg's head pounded continuously, and her stomach was queasy. She had to keep reminding herself that she hadn't done anything wrong, except for telling her parents she was spending the night with a girlfriend. They were ominously calm when she had called. It was their standard reaction to emergencies, and their quiet voices had sent a chill up her spine.

She had run out of dry clothes and had to borrow Kristin's. Stuffed into jeans too small, she could hardly breathe. It seemed to her that they should all be making timetables, comparing alibis, and exchanging theories about what happened, but she just didn't seem to have the energy to suggest it. Instead she sat, white and dazed, staring at the phone and darting uneasy glances around the room.

"My dad is going to kill me," Bryan said dismally.

It was Dusty who worried Meg most. He sat chewing on his thumbnail, and when he looked her way there was no recognition—his eyes were blank. "I'm sure the police will figure it all out," Meg said suddenly.

"All they have to figure out," said C.C., narrowing her eyes, "is which one of you murdered Rick."

"It could have been an accident," said Meg too loudly. "Somebody could have picked up the gun, and it went off by accident. Things like that happen."

There was a banging at the back door. "Police," a deep voice yelled.

Jeff smoothed his hair, blinked rapidly, and headed for the back door.

A moment later he led two police officers into the living room. "Can one of you identify the deceased?" said the tall policeman.

"We all knew him," Jeff said. "He was Rick Eason, the tennis pro at North Hills Country Club."

"Do you have any idea what he was doing out here?" asked the tall cop.

"I invited him," said C.C.

"We were having a birthday party for Dusty," Meg added. "No one had any reason to kill Rick. I think it must have been an accident. I'm sure it was."

The officers' faces were pictures of skepticism. When they took everyone's names and addresses Meg saw the short man's head jerk up at Dusty's name. The officer's pale blue eyes fixed implacably on Dusty's face, and Meg knew he had to be thinking that Dusty had discovered another body only weeks before. Another "accident."

The questioning that followed was nightmarish for Meg. Another police officer arrived who seemed to rank higher than the first two. Once he arrived they lost no time in separating the kids. The tallest officer directed Meg and Kristin to sit at opposite ends of the living room while the others were taken off to different parts of the house.

Meg was vaguely conscious of the arrival of more police. She could hear people moving around in the kitchen, and she thought she could make out the crackle of a police radio in the background. The tall police officer fixed Meg with a stern look. "Do your parents know you're here?"

That shook her confidence, but she clung stubbornly to the story she had decided on—they were having a quiet little birthday party and had all gotten ready for bed early after the cake and the scavenger hunt. It was obvious that the officer didn't believe her, but Meg just kept telling herself that her story was basically true, and she refused to budge from it.

The officer seemed extremely interested in how well each of them knew Rick Eason. Luckily Meg had nothing to conceal on that score. She could truthfully say that most of them hardly knew him. No, no one had quarreled with him, she insisted. No, as far as she knew he had no enemies. No, there were no problems.

"I wonder where my parents are," Meg said anxiously. "I thought they'd be here by now."

"I expect all the parents are waiting outside," said the officer. "We can't have people tromping through a crime scene."

He went on with his questioning. It was just a quiet little party, Meg repeated. Perhaps she hadn't thought it was such a good idea to have it out in the country with no chaperons, but that was the way Dusty wanted it, and she had wanted to help cheer him up.

The officer played with his ballpoint pen—click, click, click. "His sister was killed just a few weeks ago, wasn't she? I seem to remember it was a case sort of like this one."

"Elizabeth's death was an accident," Meg said. "The gun went off in her hands."

"You seem to be a pretty accident-prone bunch of kids." He rolled up a stick of gum and popped it into his mouth. Meg watched the working of his jaw with morbid fascination. "Do you have any idea who fired the fatal shot?" he asked.

"No!" she cried.

He went down his list of names. He wanted to know where everybody had been when Meg heard the shot. She explained they were spread out all over the house. No, she insisted, she didn't think it was peculiar. They were getting ready for bed.

She began to feel numb from the endless questions. Did her answers make sense? She couldn't tell anymore. She felt insulted by the implication that she was a wild party animal, but she didn't know what to do about it. She wished she could show him all her Good Citizenship certificates from grade school.

At last, to her relief, the officer turned his attention to Kristin, who sat cowering at the dining room table.

Meg couldn't hear much of what Kristin was telling him, which was probably what he had had in mind when he instructed the girls to sit far apart, but she decided it didn't much matter. She had told him her story, and she was going to stick to it.

Now that she was out from under the pressure of questions, Meg found herself wondering uneasily where Dusty had been when the shot was fired. He said he'd been at the boat house. Could he have tiptoed in the back door, grabbed the gun off the table, and shot Rick? She wished she'd noticed whether the kitchen floor was wet before they all tracked mud in when they had come in from finding Rick's body. Now there was no telling if Dusty had come in and left a trail of mud earlier. She pressed her fingers to her aching temples. She knew she had to stop thinking like that. Dusty had no reason to kill Rick. It was Bryan he suspected of murdering Elizabeth, not Rick. Suddenly Meg darted a frightened glance at the police officer. Out of the whirlpool of confused thoughts and bewildering, half-understood incidents, one detail rose ominously to the top of her mind. Rick was wearing Bryan's raincoat! The significance of this appalled her. In dim light Dusty might easily have mistaken Rick for Bryan!

While Meg sat frozen by this awful thought the other kids were being ushered through the living room by the police. She jumped up. "Do we get to go home now?"

The answer was no. There would be more questions at the station. The police shepherded them outside into the drizzle. Beyond the flashing blue light of the police car with its crackling radio Meg could make out her parents sitting in their car. At that point her self-control snapped, and she ran toward them, sobbing.

13

It was dawn by the time Meg got home. No longer able to remember precisely what she had told the police, she had a knot of fear in her stomach that would not go away. In the car on the way home she had told her parents as much as she could remember about what the police had asked, and over and over she recounted what had happened after she heard the shot.

"Maybe we should get a lawyer." Dr. Redding frowned. "This sounds really bad to me."

"But I haven't done anything wrong!" cried Meg. "I was just an innocent bystander."

"Meg's right," said Mrs. Redding. "It's all horrible, but she's just a witness, not a suspect."

"I don't like it," said Dr. Redding.

As soon as they got back to the house Meg unplugged the phone by her bed and fell into an exhausted sleep.

Afternoon sun was streaming in her bedroom window when her mother came in to wake her. "Phone for you." Mrs. Redding's expression was troubled. "I think it's C.C."

Meg groaned and reached for the receiver. "Hullo?" she said before remembering she had unplugged the phone the night before. She groped drowsily for the jack and plugged it back in. "Hello?" she repeated.

"Hi. It's me," said C.C.

Meg suddenly sat bolt upright. "C.C.," she said urgently, "what did you tell the police?"

"The truth," said C.C.

"Oh, no!" Meg groaned. She could just imagine their reaction to the story that Dusty had hidden a gun in the boat house.

"Look, don't you want them to catch Rick's murderer?" demanded C.C.

"I'm not sure."

"Then we don't have anything to talk about," C.C. said coldly.

"I mean of course I want them to catch the murderer, if there *is* a murderer. I'm just so afraid they're going to get the wrong idea. I feel sure it was an accident. Somebody must have picked up the gun, and it went off accidentally. And now he's afraid to admit it."

"Grow up, Meg. This wasn't any accident."

"It could have been."

"Like Elizabeth's death was an accident?"

Meg sucked in her breath.

"Guns don't go off by themselves," said C.C. "Somebody murdered Rick."

"C.C.," Meg asked anxiously, "did they ask you anything about Elizabeth?"

"Sure. Figure it out for yourself—Elizabeth and Rick were killed with the same gun."

"Do we know that for sure?"

"I don't have a ballistics report, if that's what you're asking. But Jeff said it was the same gun, and I believe him."

Meg picked up her alarm clock and stared at it in disbelief. Could it really be three in the afternoon? "I'd better call Dusty."

"Forget it. You won't get through. I tried, but his father answered the phone. He must have flown back into town this morning. I guess his secretary or somebody finally managed to get in touch with him. He said Dusty was still sleeping, but I didn't believe it. He knows how bad it looks for Dusty, and doesn't want him talking to anybody. If Mr. Ellis weren't a hotshot lawyer and a prominent citizen, they would have arrested Dusty already. Think about it, Meg. Dusty put an ad in the school paper inviting us all to a murder. We get there, and sure enough, there's a murder right on schedule, just the way he promised. It's open and shut. Every angle leads to him. Who planned the party? Dusty. Who did the gun belong to? Dusty. Who brought it out to the reservoir? Dusty. And who happened to discover Elizabeth's body when she was killed by the same gun just a few weeks ago? Dusty."

"Don't talk that way, C.C." Meg's fingers tightened on the receiver. "Dusty didn't do it." She swallowed. "Do you think this phone can be tapped? Maybe we'd better talk in French."

"My French isn't too hot," said C.C. "Maybe you'd better come over to my house if you want to talk."

Meg dressed hastily and grabbed a doughnut from the kitchen counter. "I'm going over to C.C.'s, Mom."

"Meg, don't you think we ought to talk?"

"We've already talked!" wailed Meg. "I told you everything! I need to find out what C.C. told the police. You know her. She'll say any old thing that comes into her head. I just hope she didn't give the police the wrong idea."

"I don't think you should go out right now. If you want to talk to C.C., do it on the phone."

"I'm afraid the phone might be tapped."

"What do you care? You don't have anything to hide." Her mother's eyes were anxious. "Do you?"

"Of course I don't have anything to hide! It's Dusty I'm worried about."

"Dusty has something to hide?"

"Oh, I don't know!" Meg exploded. "I won't be long, Mom. Honest."

"Margaret Emily, you don't seem to realize how serious a matter this is. You lied to us. You are involved—completely innocently, of course, but still involved—in a serious crime."

"I realize that. I do, honestly. But that's why I've got to talk to C.C."

It took five minutes of pleading before her mother finally gave in. Meg grabbed the car keys off the rack and took off.

At the Carmodys' house she found C.C. sitting on her bed, sorting through the contents of a cardboard box. With a weary flick of her wrist she flipped a shiny plastic card onto the bedspread, and a tin of aspirin fell to the bed with a rattle. Sunlight streamed in the window, adding fiery highlights to her dark hair and casting her eyes in shadow. Meg couldn't guess what she was thinking. C.C. kept tossing small objects onto the bed as if they were cards in some strange version of poker, but her face showed no signs of animation or even of life.

"I swear your mother looks like she's been tearing her hair out," said Meg, closing the door behind her.

"She thinks I killed Rick," said C.C. dully. "That's the worst thing that could possibly happen, so of course she's convinced it *has* happened. I keep trying to tell her that it's Dusty the police are interested in."

"Do you really think they suspect him?" Meg regarded her anxiously. "What makes you think that? Did they say so?"

"They didn't have to. It doesn't take much brain power to figure out what they thought of him shoving evidence down the garbage disposal just before they got there."

"Who told them that?" gasped Meg.

"I did. No point looking at me that way, Meg. I knew Kristin was bound to tell them, so even if I

wanted to, it wouldn't make sense to lie about it."
C.C. dumped the entire contents of the cardboard
box onto her bed. A bottle of Extra-strength
Excedrin bounced off the bed and onto the floor.
When Meg retrieved it and replaced it she saw that
a collection of laminated drivers' licenses was lying
on the bedspread. She picked one up. "Richard
Hardy?" She glanced at C.C. "But this has a picture
of Rick!"

"Turns out he had several different licenses."
C.C. tossed another license in her direction. "This
one's for Richard Easterberg and makes him five
years older. It must have been his fake ID when he
was a teenager. I figure he kept it for sentimental
reasons." C.C. leaned back against the headboard.
"Is this grim or what? The club called me right after
lunch and asked me to come clean out his locker.
He'd put me down as next of kin! Can you believe
that?" She glanced at the closed bedroom door.
"You can bet I didn't tell Mom that. She's freaking
out enough as it is."

"What's this?" Meg picked up a videocassette.
"Dirty movies?"

"Very funny. It's the video of the demonstration
match he did when they were having that round
robin tournament at the club. Rick was always
trying to improve his game." With a wry twist of
her mouth C.C. flipped a driver's license aside. "To
tell you the truth, I was getting tired of Rick." She
sighed. "But when I look at all this stuff—it's sad.
Like this Excedrin—he had migraines, you know.
It's like this is all there is left of his life, just this

junk from his locker." She stiffened suddenly and paled. "God, you don't think they're going to expect me to arrange the funeral!"

"Well, they can't make you. You weren't married to him." Meg hesitated. "Were you?"

"Gosh, no! Of course not! I can't believe this," wailed C.C. "This is absolutely the worst year of my whole life. I might as well change my name and start over somewhere else."

"That seems to have been Rick's approach," said Meg dryly. "You don't really think Dusty killed him, do you, C.C.?"

"Well, no," C.C. admitted grudgingly. "But if Dusty didn't, who did?"

"Look, you're the one who knew Rick best. If he had any enemies, you'd be the one to know."

C.C. shook her head.

"No old girlfriends?" prodded Meg. "No ex-wives that might have been stalking him?"

"Nobody around here."

"What about money? Maybe he lent somebody money. Maybe he borrowed some from the mob. He must have had a bank account, and I'll bet it would tell us something. If you're the next of kin, maybe you can find out what was in it."

"Forget that! Next time somebody accuses me of being the next of kin I'm going to tell them they've got the wrong girl." C.C. made a face. "Besides, Rick was always short of cash. Even if he did have a bank account, I doubt there was anything in it. A few weeks ago he did seem to have a lot of money, and I was really surprised because he was usually so short. He took me out to a fancy restaurant and said we'd be doing it a lot from then on."

"When was that? The fancy restaurant, I mean."

"I guess it was a week or so after the round robin tournaments, because while we were there Rick saw this lady who had played in the winning doubles, or whatever they called it, and he went over and congratulated her."

Meg got up and walked over to the desk to turn C.C.'s calendar back to September. "When was that? It could be important."

"I don't see how." C.C. glanced at the calendar. "See, I marked the tournaments on there. Rick was sort of working double time then—we hardly went out."

"C.C., that was the week Elizabeth was killed!"

"So what?"

"Don't you see? First Elizabeth was killed, and then all of a sudden Rick had money. What if somebody paid him to be the trigger man? What if he killed Elizabeth?"

"That's the stupidest idea I've ever heard. Why would anybody pay Rick to kill Elizabeth? It's not like she was an heiress. She was just an ordinary kid."

"I still think there's got to be a connection," Meg insisted.

"The police think there's a connection, too," said C.C. "Dusty."

"Not Dusty. A different kind of connection. I don't care what you say, Dusty didn't kill Elizabeth."

"I know you want to think that, Meg, but you have to admit he's been acting weird. All that stuff about the murder game—the gun, the voodoo doll, the ketchup trap for Bryan—you can't tell me that stuff was normal."

"Dusty didn't have any reason to shoot Elizabeth," said Meg. "They loved each other."

C.C. jumped up and began pacing the floor. Restless energy radiated from her. "Meg," she said suddenly. "Have you ever thought there's something spooky about twins?"

"No!" cried Meg. "That's ridiculous."

"In some primitive societies they kill twins at birth. It's an anthropological fact. Look it up. Maybe Dusty and Elizabeth were so close it wasn't normal. Maybe he felt she was suffocating him. It would be really easy for him to kill her, when you think about it. She trusted him. He could walk right up to her with a gun, and she'd probably just laugh."

"He was at the reservoir," put in Meg in a faint voice.

"Ever heard of cars? Suppose while his parents were lazing around reading the paper or something he says he's going out to get a loaf of bread, and he comes back to the house and murders Elizabeth."

"But Dusty thinks Bryan did it!"

"That's what Dusty *says* he thinks. What if he knows better? Because he killed her himself."

"But don't you see the whole murder party proves that Dusty suspected Bryan?" insisted Meg. "The whole stupid game was designed to get on

Bryan's nerves so he'd crack and confess to murdering Elizabeth—the gun in the boat house, the tape recorder whispering 'I know what you did.' It was all supposed to get to Bryan."

"Well, it got to us all, didn't it? Looks like Dusty succeeded beyond his wildest dreams. Believe me, Kristin nearly cracked up when we found that voodoo doll and then the lights went out, and I have to admit I wasn't all that calm myself."

"Dusty wasn't really sure who killed Elizabeth, so he tried pointing the finger at other people, too. But I'm sure Bryan was his main suspect."

"That's only because Bryan is such a jerk," said C.C. "He'd be anybody's main suspect. But can you see Bryan having the guts to kill anybody?"

Meg had to agree it was hard to imagine. "C.C." she began hesitantly, "Dusty says this mysterious girl used to come and see Elizabeth sometimes."

C.C. gave a short laugh. "So we're falling back on the mysterious stranger, huh? Just keep in mind you've only got Dusty's word for the girl. And there sure wasn't any mysterious girl out at the lake last night."

"But what if Roxy were the mysterious girl?"

C.C. stared. "What are you getting at?"

Meg quickly sketched in her theory about Roxy for C.C. and was disappointed when C.C. giggled. "It's ridiculous, Meg. Listen to yourself. Have you found anybody who ever saw this 'mysterious girl' except Dusty? Sounds to me like it's an obvious attempt by Dusty to divert suspicion from himself."

"I could ask around," said Meg. "If Hilary and Elizabeth went shopping together, somebody must have seen them."

"Sure," said C.C. mockingly.

"Unless they went shopping in Raleigh."

"Just can't let go of your nice little theory, can you?" C.C.'s dark eyes bored into Meg's. "I'll give you a better theory. Maybe Dusty went nuts and was so confused he couldn't tell Bryan from Rick. Maybe he shot Rick by mistake."

"Dusty isn't nuts." Meg stood up suddenly. C.C. was getting uncomfortably close to voicing Meg's own fears. Meg had a horrible feeling that if she wasn't careful, she would end up blurting out that Rick had been wearing Bryan's raincoat. "I better get on home. My mother didn't even want to let me come over here."

C.C. fell back on her bed, and the Excedrin bottle bounced. Her arms went limp, and she suddenly looked exhausted. "When it comes to freaking out, believe me, my mom's way ahead of her."

Meg couldn't shake the idea that Elizabeth's murder and Rick's were connected. Driving home, she kept turning the facts over and over in her mind. Rick had money right after Elizabeth died, and it had to be significant that Rick and Elizabeth were killed with the same gun. She was sure Elizabeth's death must have been where it all began. The trouble was, she had no idea who shot Elizabeth.

Her hands tightened on the steering wheel. All

right, she told herself, suppose the mysterious girl had killed Elizabeth. And suppose that mysterious girl was Roxy, and suppose she did have a good reason to want Elizabeth dead. Why would Roxy then want to kill Rick? Did he know? Was he blackmailing her? The tennis court was so close to Dusty's house that it was possible Rick had seen the murderer come and go. But even if he saw the disguised Roxy, how could he possibly guess who she was? Meg wasn't even sure Rick had met Roxy before they went out to the reservoir together. It was pretty absurd to think he could have recognized her and started blackmailing her. Or was it? Meg sucked in her breath suddenly. The car. Roxy would have had to drive a car to the house, wouldn't she? Cars were so much easier to identify than people—they had license plates. Suppose she hadn't parked in front of the house. Suppose she had parked at the country club so the car wouldn't be seen at the house. And suppose Rick had seen it all, had seen a flashily dressed girl park at the club and walk to Dusty's house, had written down the license number, or remembered it, and when Elizabeth's death was announced had traced Roxy and blackmailed her. Meg's head was spinning when she pulled into her own driveway. Theories. Nothing but theories. She needed proof.

14

When Dusty showed up at his locker Monday morning Meg couldn't remember any of the questions she had planned to ask him. "I hope Grunwald will take my algebra homework late," he said. His smile was wan.

"Dusty, are you okay?" It was a stupid question. He looked terrible.

"My dad thinks we should retain outside counsel." Dusty pulled his books out of the locker. "That means he thinks it's real bad. I'm not supposed to talk to anybody about what happened. I guess you realize they got hold of my ad in the newspaper—'You're invited to a murder.' You can imagine what it was like trying to explain that. I tried to tell them that it was just a stupid game. But with you and Bryan finding the gun in the boat house—well, it looks bad for me." Dusty licked his lips. "I told them the gun wasn't loaded. I said,

119

'Man, I wouldn't bring a loaded gun to a party. You think I'm nuts?' It's true, too, Meg. I made sure the clip was empty before I packed up the gun."

"Then how—"

"Turns out that when you fire a semiautomatic, another bullet automatically moves up into firing position. Dad explained that to me last night. So the clip can be empty and the thing still be ready to fire."

"You mean it had a bullet in it that you didn't know about?"

"Yeah, and that's all it took, isn't it?" He shook his head. "Jeez, I don't understand it! Who could have killed Rick? Do you think it was C.C.?"

Meg remembered the melancholy way C.C. had sorted over Rick's few effects. "I really don't think so," she said.

"But the rest of us hardly even knew him. I mean, you don't go shooting somebody just because he's obnoxious. Probably the only reason the police haven't arrested me is they can't figure out my motive. I'd have to be absolutely out of my mind to murder Rick." He managed a smile. "So I'm just concentrating on looking very, very sane."

The bell rang with a nerve-jangling clang, and they hurried to homeroom. Meg found that she had been comforted by her short talk with Dusty. He did seem sane. All those people telling her that he was cracking up had probably affected her more than she realized, but he only sounded worried and upset, which was absolutely normal.

In homeroom Mrs. Brownlee began reading a list

of announcements. "So, how was your Sunday?" Jeff whispered to Meg.

"Not so good."

"I bet mine was worse. After the police quit grilling me, my dad started."

"Jeff, have the police found out anything? Have they done any checking into Rick's background?"

"You don't think they'd tell me, do you? No, siree. I have to answer the questions. I don't get to ask any. I have, according to Dad, forfeited all my human rights by putting him in such an embarrassing situation."

"But you must know something," said Meg desperately. "Do the police think Dusty did it?"

Jeff glanced over at Dusty. "I'm afraid so."

The bell rang, and Meg fought her way through the crowd of kids surging out of the classroom and managed to grab Dusty's hand.

"Hey, Dusty, Meg, what's this I hear about C.C.'s boyfriend getting himself shot?" Craig Weathers had caught up with them. In a minute Meg and Dusty found themselves surrounded by curious classmates.

"I don't know anything," Dusty said wearily. "We were having a party out at the reservoir, and late at night C.C.'s boyfriend went outside. That's where we found his body, and that's all we know."

"Maybe it was one of those serial killers that did it," said Muriel Fuerst. "Did you see that movie *The Hitchhiker* on channel two? It was really creepy. This guy went all over the country shooting people at random."

"It could have been deer hunters." David Miller pushed his glasses back up on his nose. "You can get shot by one of those guys from a mile away. They don't even know they've hit anybody with their high-powered rifles. There ought to be a law."

By afternoon Meg was aware that a different theory had been spread around school. People stopped talking whenever she went up to them. She heard the sibilant hiss of whispers and sensed people staring at her. When she ran into Dusty in the parking lot after school her ears were burning.

"I'd love to kill that Kristin," she said bitterly. "She's spreading rumors all over school."

"Watch what you say," said Dusty. "What if it's Kristin's body we find next?"

"What a creepy thing to say!"

"I can't help it. I seem to be getting the bad habit of discovering bodies lately."

"Dusty, we've got to talk. I have an idea."

"What? Believe me, I could use a good idea."

Meg could feel herself blushing. "It sounds kind of silly, but I'd really like to talk to you about it. I mean, I think if we can go over it together, it may not turn out to be as silly as it seems at first."

He looked puzzled. "Well, sure. Why don't you come on over to the house?"

15

As Meg pulled her car into Dusty's driveway she glanced over at the country club, where a couple of trim white-haired ladies were playing tennis. Across the street the Ellises' neighbors had stacked bales of hay and pumpkins in a colorful seasonal display. In every direction the neighborhood was neat and well kept. But at Dusty's house there were subtle signs of neglect. The geraniums in the planters on the front steps had drooped, blackened by frost, and the flowers in the hanging basket by the front door were withered.

Dusty unlocked the front door and threw it open. "I hope this is going to be good, Meg."

Meg smiled nervously, remembering how C.C. had giggled at her theory. At least she could be sure Dusty wouldn't do that. He didn't look as if he had a laugh left in him. He led her back to the kitchen and took a two-liter bottle of soda pop out of the fridge. "I'm supposed to sit here in the house and not go anywhere or talk to anybody. Dad's afraid I'm going to say something incriminating. He's out meeting up with an old law school buddy, or he'd be here now keeping an eye on me. Have the cops been by your house?"

"Twice," Meg admitted. "They explained to me what 'accessory after the fact' means. It's sort of like an accomplice, and they implied I am one."

"You think you've got it bad? I'm suspect number one. Those cops' mouths water when they look at me. Why do you think Dad's out with Barney Hudson? It's because Barney's the best criminal lawyer in this part of the state. The two of them are probably busy plotting my defense right now." He took a deep breath. "You know what they do to convicted murderers these days? Lethal injection. They just give you a shot, and you quit breathing. I swear sometimes that sounds pretty good to me. It really does."

"Stop it, Dusty! That's sick!"

"I can't help it. Every time I think my life can't get any worse, something else happens—and it's worse."

"There must be something we can do! Look, remember when you told me about the mysterious girl who used to visit Elizabeth sometimes?"

"Yeah." He frowned. "What about it?"

"Suppose the mysterious girl was Roxy in disguise."

"Why would Roxy put on a disguise? If she

wanted to see Elizabeth, nobody would stop her from coming over."

"But suppose she was planning a murder! If Roxy always came over to see Elizabeth, she might be a suspect. But if whenever she came over she was in disguise, nobody could possibly connect her with the murder. Even if she were seen coming to the house on the very day Elizabeth was killed, it wouldn't matter. Nobody would connect that weird-looking girl with Roxy." Meg began to speak more quickly. "What hit me was that the girl you described was the exact opposite of Roxy. Roxy's real blond. If she wore a black wig, she wouldn't look like herself at all because the first thing you notice about her is that she's so blond. Also, you said this mysterious girl wore heaps of makeup. That sounds like a disguise right there. Did you ever actually get up close to this girl? I mean, like talk to her?"

"No, not to *talk* to her. Maybe once or twice Elizabeth said, 'We're off, folks,' and the other girl wouldn't say anything, or maybe just a few words, like"—he pitched his voice high—"'Yes, we'll be going.' Weird-sounding, somehow." He frowned.

"Roxy won a contest one time as a ventriloquist. Tell me, Dusty. Did anybody else see her?"

"Maybe Mom. That's not much help, is it?"

Meg sighed. "It would be better if it were somebody outside your family. I mean, the police aren't likely to pay too much attention if you and your mom start talking about a mysterious stranger at this point. I wonder where Elizabeth and this girl went. If it was here in town, then somebody must have seen them. I mean, Elizabeth would have run into heaps of people she knew at the mall."

"I have the idea sometimes they went to Raleigh. Maybe they went to some offbeat movies there or something." It was a long-standing gripe with film buffs that the local mall played only top-grossing mainstream movies. "I just caught glimpses of them coming and going once or twice, you know? It's not like they were here that much. I had the feeling maybe they were trying to avoid me. Usually Elizabeth's friends would sort of hang around more. Like they'd come in and pass the time of day with Mom or me, flop on the living room couch, check out my CDs, that kind of thing. This girl just darted in and out. That's why I said she was mysterious."

"Do you think it could have been Roxy?"

"I don't know, Meg. I don't think so. I only saw the girl a few times, but I have the idea she had a funny way of walking and a funny voice. She was so *weird,* and Roxy isn't weird. I wish I could remember better. At the time it just seemed like one of Elizabeth's strange friends." He shrugged almost imperceptibly. "Like Bryan. Who could ever figure out what she saw in Bryan? And remember Sue-Sue Menken? The girl who shaved her head. Boy, was I glad when she moved away."

"The point is, Roxy could probably act weird if she put her mind to it. Don't you think?"

"I guess. One time I remember in particular this

girl and Elizabeth were dressed up so it looked like they were going to a costume party, with those black stockings with criss-cross threads—"

"Fishnet stockings?"

"I guess. They looked like girls in an old western dance hall. I just happened to get a peek at the way they were dressed before they left. They sneaked out of the house with raincoats wrapped around them."

"Who do we know who's had a costume party lately?"

"Nobody. It's hopeless. Nobody saw this girl but me, and maybe Mom. Even if your theory is absolutely right, we're never going to get any proof."

"There's got to be somebody who saw them together."

"Maybe, but we'll never find them. And I can't even think straight, I'm under so much pressure. I swear, Dad is acting like he thinks I killed Rick! I wish to heaven I'd never had that stupid party."

"I'm going to ask around."

"Maybe you'd better drop it, Meg. You might just make things worse."

Meg snorted. "I don't see how things could get any worse."

"Well, they haven't arrested me. That's something. Maybe we ought to leave well enough alone. Not that I expect you to listen to me. You're the most pig-headed person I know." He sounded tired as he walked her out to the car and opened the door for her. When he bent to kiss her his lips were cold and Meg found herself thinking of Elizabeth. She shivered.

Meg had caught Dusty's mood of black hopelessness. As she drove away it seemed perfectly likely to her that Dusty was going to be tried for murder, and maybe even convicted. Her chest was so constricted she could hardly breathe, and she gritted her teeth, trying to keep from screaming. She knew she ought to go home, but instead drove to C.C.'s house on automatic pilot. To her relief, it was C.C. who answered the door.

"Who do we know that works in the mall?" Meg asked her urgently. "Preferably in someplace central and with a good view."

"Angela Freeman works at the snack shop by the fountain. Used to, anyway."

"I don't know her, do I?"

"Sure you do. She was in our typing class last year. She sat right next to you. She's a friend of Kristin, as a matter of fact, which sort of makes me wonder about her."

"I think I'll give her a call."

"Why? What's this all about, Meg?"

"Let's just call it my investigation. Let me have that box of Rick's things, too."

"What for? There's nothing in there. Just aspirin, athlete's foot medicine, and stuff."

"There has to be something," said Meg desperately. "I've got to explore every lead. I've got to find out who really committed these murders!"

"You've been reading too many Nancy Drews,"

said C. C. "You're losing it, Meg, old girl." But she went to her bedroom and got the box.

Meg waited at home until the mall closed at nine before calling Angela Freeman. When she heard the voice on the other end of the line she suddenly remembered the face of the thin, earnest girl who had sat next to her in typing class. When asked, Angela admitted she had probably seen Elizabeth at the mall a couple of times, but couldn't remember seeing her with any weird-looking girl. She assured Meg she was too busy selling fudge to check on who was hanging out. She supposed she would have noticed if Elizabeth had been with somebody besides her usual crowd. But why? Angela was suddenly curious. Did this have something to do with the murder?

"Maybe." Meg toyed with the leaves of the philodendron trailing from the brass planter in the kitchen window. Her mom's stupid philodendron was getting out of hand, starting to look like the plant that ate Philadelphia. But then everything was somehow sinister to her these days. Even the pots her mother had hanging on the pegboard in the kitchen were beginning to look like lethal weapons. "I'm trying to do a little detective work," she said. "Maybe I'll end up helping out the police. Would you mind asking around for me? If anybody saw Elizabeth with a weird-looking girl, I want to know about it."

"I'll take my yearbook to work and show everybody Elizabeth's picture," said Angela. "You think this mysterious girl murdered Elizabeth?"

"Could be. I'm just checking out every lead."

"Who killed the tennis pro, then? Kristin said nobody was out at the reservoir but you guys."

"Anybody could get in a car and drive out. Rick didn't necessarily have to be killed by somebody who was in the house," hedged Meg. She certainly didn't want to tell Angela her theory about the mysterious girl being Roxy in disguise. The last thing she needed was for word of her suspicions to get back to Roxy.

"This is so exciting!" squealed Angela. "I'll ask around."

16

The next morning was gloomy, and Meg's spirits sagged to fit the weather. She was wondering if she had figured it all wrong. Her idea about the mysterious girl seemed so bizarre. Maybe the reason Roxy as the murderer appealed to her was that she just didn't like Roxy. It was a good enough theory, though—it all fit together. But there were problems with it. If Roxy wanted Elizabeth dead, wouldn't there have been a simpler way for her to do it than by constructing an elaborate false identity? The more Meg thought about it, the more her theory seemed insubstantial, like a wisp of smoke.

She shook the rain off her umbrella and stuffed it into her locker. Then she sped off to homeroom, scarcely noticing whom she passed.

The first bell had rung, and the hall was filled with kids rushing in all directions. Their hurrying bodies gave off the smell of wet tennis shoes. Feeling a faint sense of disgust at so much crowded-together humanity, the murderer slammed the locker closed and watched Meg walk away.

Meg was getting too close. Stiflingly close. Dangerously close. She would insist on poking around. It was all over school that she was conducting a full-scale investigation. Everything had been going so well until she stuck her nose in. And there was no way to make her stop. No matter what anybody said to her, she barrelled ahead, not paying a bit of attention. She was going to have to be stopped. It would be awful to kill her, and the nightmares would get even worse afterward—but it had to be done.

When Meg got to Mrs. Brownlee's room she tossed her books down and slid into her desk. Jeff was in his place but obviously avoiding her. Looking at him with his head down, so determinedly shunning her, Meg grew cold. Dusty was right. The police were waiting for the chance to arrest Dusty, and Jeff knew it. That was why he couldn't look at her.

When Dusty came in just before the final bell he seemed to be defeated. Meg didn't try to catch up with him after homeroom. What was the use? She didn't have anything useful to offer him. Meg spotted Roxy in the hall and instinctively shied away from her. She was so keyed up she felt as if she were balancing on a knife's edge. She took off at once in the other direction, but somehow Roxy managed to struggle past the bunch of sophomores who were blocking the hallway and catch up with her.

"Meg!" Roxy's smile was strangely fixed. "So—how's it going?"

"Okay," Meg said, edging away from her.

"What I really mean is how's the murder investigation going?" Roxy twirled a strand of her pale hair around her finger. "C.C. told me you took this box full of Rick's things back to your house. She said you were going to do the Nancy Drew bit and unmask the murderer. She did a great imitation of you at the Pizza Hut last night and had the whole place in hysterics. Kristin practically fell off her chair."

"I didn't realize I was being so funny." Meg swallowed. The last thing she wanted was to stand in the hall discussing the murder with Roxy.

"Jeff didn't think it was funny either, but C.C. was laughing herself sick."

"You'd think having two people killed would get her down."

"*Two?*" Roxy stopped in her tracks. "But I thought Elizabeth's death was an accident. The police said it was. I saw it in the paper."

"I guess." Meg wanted to get away from those pale eyes and the tense smile. "I don't know anything, really. You probably know more than I do. Jeff is the one with the cop in the family."

"Jeff won't tell me anything," said Roxy in a tight voice.

Meg turned and fled into her next class. She

didn't even care if Roxy realized she was avoiding her.

The school day seemed interminably long. It was hopeless for Meg to concentrate on algebra or history or English when her mind was a kaleidoscope of jumbled scenes from the weekend, kaleidoscope images that didn't add up but wouldn't stop nagging at her. She remembered the gun in the boathouse, the screams in the night, and Rick's body lying in the mud.

When Meg got home that day after school the house was oppressively empty. She fixed herself a cheese sandwich and transported it from the kitchen to the adjoining family room. There she sat cross-legged on the floor and sorted through Rick's personal effects. She wasn't hopeful about finding anything, but it gave her something to do to keep her from screaming, which was the main thing. Meg was desperate.

"Somewhere there has to be a pattern," she muttered, "if I can just find it." If the mysterious girl was a false trail, there must be some other trail that would lead her to a solution. It was a problem, she thought, not unlike the problems on an algebra test. Some things she knew, and others were unknown quantities—x's and y's. If she took the puzzle piece by piece and carefully checked all her answers, she might surprise herself by getting the right one.

She began by tasting every single tablet in Rick's aspirin bottle, but they all turned out to be aspirin, and she had to go wash out her mouth out afterward. Then she sniffed at the athlete's foot remedy. It smelled exactly like her father's athlete's foot remedy. She wasn't sure what she was looking for, but she felt that if she could only find something suspicious, it might be the clue that would lead her to the murderer. She ran her fingers along the edges of the laminated drivers' licenses, but there was no hidden slit. Not that she had any idea what could have been hidden inside a dirver's license, except perhaps a microchip, and she wasn't sure she'd know a microchip if she found one.

Everything in the cardboard box was disappointingly ordinary. Meg hadn't had much hope of finding anything to begin with, so she wasn't even very disappointed. Having nothing else to do, she put Rick's tennis video in the VCR and switched on the TV.

She could feel her afternoon snack gurgling uncomfortably in her stomach as she watched Rick demonstrate his powerful backhand. It was strange to see a small image of him bounding across the television screen when the image of him that she carried in her mind was so much more real and powerful—the one of his broad back straining the material of Bryan's raincoat, his hair soaked and parted in back by the pounding rain, the neat black hole in the raincoat where his life had leaked out. Meg realized that she had been staring at the screen for some minutes as if in a trance. She hadn't really seen anything, yet she had the uncomfortable feeling that something was wrong. She got up from the floor, rewound the tape, and played it again. The tape sputtered a bit, then Rick's arm went high over his head once more in a serve. There was nothing odd about it, yet she had the nagging feeling she was missing something. She rewound the tape and tried again. Perhaps it was her imagination, she thought, and then she saw it—Bryan's car. The video camera trained on Rick gave a view of Dusty's house beyond the courts. In the driveway was Bryan's car. Meg stared at it, disbelieving.

She ejected the tape and checked the label— "Demonstration Match." It was labeled carefully in small block letters—and dated. It was the date of Elizabeth's death.

She pounced on the phone and dialed Dusty's number. To her relief, he answered right away. "I've got the proof!" she cried. "I know who killed Elizabeth! It's in a video done on the day of the murder." Her voice sank to a whisper. "I can see Bryan's car in your driveway."

"You're kidding me."

"I can even read the numbers on his license plate."

"I'm coming right over."

Dusty was not supposed to come over when Meg's parents were at work, but it seemed silly to worry about that when a murder case was breaking wide open. Minutes later Meg let him in the front door. "Let me see it," he said abruptly.

He perched on the arm of the family room couch as she played the video for him. "I thought he was there, and he was." Dusty's voice was cold. "I'm going to kill the creep."

"Oh, Dusty, hush. You are not!"

"You're right. I'm not." Dusty banged on the upholstery with his fist. "I can't believe that we've actually got proof he was there." Dusty was pale. "The mysterious girl didn't have anything to do with it after all."

"We've got important evidence," said Meg. "We'd better call the police right away. If something happened to this tape, we wouldn't have a bit of proof." She leafed through the phone book, found the number of the police station, and dialed it. A woman with a high-pitched nasal voice said, "Can you hold, please?" and music began playing. "I can't believe this," said Meg crossly. "They've put me on hold. I should have dialed nine-one-one."

The doorbell pinged. "I'll get it." Dusty leapt up and went to answer the door.

"Whoever heard of the police putting you on hold when you're about to pounce on a murderer?" grumbled Meg under her breath. "Who is it, Dusty?" she called. He didn't answer. She pressed the speaker phone button to keep the line open and put the receiver back on the rack. "Dusty?" She took a step toward the foyer.

Suddenly Bryan stepped into the kitchen–family room doorway. The hair on the back of Meg's neck stood on end when she realized he was pointing a gun at her. Not taking her eyes off him, she quietly backed away. She could still escape. There had to be a way to get out. Unfortunately, Bryan was standing between her and the door from the kitchen to the carport. "What did you do to Dusty?" she asked hoarsely.

"Don't move," he yelled, "or I'll shoot! Don't move another inch."

Meg sucked her breath in so sharply she was afraid she would choke. In a couple of long steps Bryan strode right up to her, and she was staring into the black muzzle of his gun. The gun shook slightly, and Meg held her breath, praying that it wouldn't go off in her face. She felt frozen, unable to speak. She could see that Bryan's upper lip was beaded with sweat, and she wondered briefly if he was out of his mind.

"Turn around," he said.

Meg swallowed painfully, afraid she couldn't move. She stared at him mutely for a moment.

"Do you think I'm kidding?" he snarled. "You heard me."

His face was rigid and his eyes glazed, as if he were seeing far off to another world. With horror she realized that Bryan's face might be the last thing she ever saw.

"Bryan, have you hurt Dusty? Where is he?"

Bryan chuckled. "He's out for a while. Maybe forever. The stupid idiot tried to rush me when he saw the gun. What's he doing here, anyway? You were supposed to be here by yourself." He sounded aggrieved.

Meg stared down at Bryan's gun and knew she

couldn't try rushing him. More than anything she wanted to live. Even if only for a minute or two longer.

"Why couldn't you mind your own business?" he said thickly. "Why can't everybody mind his own business? Like Elizabeth. I was sick of the way she kept criticizing me and telling me what to do. I set it up to meet her at her house on Saturday. I told her we'd have the whole weekend together. But really I sneaked away from my folks for just a couple of hours to have a serious talk with her, in private. I had thought it was time we went out with other people and asked her to stay home from the lake so we could talk. But when she found out what was on my mind she got mad—real mad." He shook his head. "She said she was going to tell."

"Tell what?" Meg's breathing was irregular, but she had a single thought in her mind—if she could keep Bryan talking, maybe Dusty would come to and go for help. "What was she going to tell, Bryan?"

He frowned. "It's so stupid. It was just a dumb game. But if my dad found out, he would have hit the roof. He's always wanting Mom and me to give out this perfect public image. Neither of us can step out of line, even for a minute. He'd have made my life hell if he found out what I'd been doing."

"What was it?"

"Nothing, really. Elizabeth and me used to drive to Raleigh to go see the *Rocky Horror Picture Show*. You know, there's a theater there that shows it all the time. It's like a ritual. A tradition. People get dressed up, and there's a stage show—you know. It's kind of raunchy." He licked his lips. "It was a chance for me to get away where nobody knew who I was. I could really let my hair down and forget about being the stupid senator's son just for once."

Meg blinked. *"You* were the mysterious girlfriend."

Bryan laughed shortly. "Dusty remembered seeing me, huh? Jeez, it was funny going over to Elizabeth's house all dressed up. I had to be careful to sneak in and out because if Dusty had got a good look at me, he'd have recognized me. That would have been okay, I guess. Heck, he wouldn't have cared if Elizabeth and me wanted to get dressed up all crazy and go freak out in Raleigh, but I couldn't risk it, because if my dad ever found out, he'd go nuts. Absolutely nuts." Bryan paled. "I couldn't take the chance."

"So that's why you killed Elizabeth?" Meg consciously tried to make her voice soothing. Surely Dusty must regain consciousness soon, she thought. Unless his skull was fractured. Meg could feel her throat closing off with fear.

"Elizabeth was acting crazy." Bryan's brow was furrowed. "It wasn't my fault. She got that gun of her dad's and said she'd never let me go. It scared me. And when she started saying that stuff about how maybe my dad ought to know about our little trips to Raleigh, maybe it'd be good to clear the air—" He choked on a sob. "God, can you believe she said that? Clear the air? I just had to shut her up. I grabbed the gun and—I shut her up. I didn't really want to kill her. I mean I didn't really mean for it to be permanent." He shook his head. "It's hard to explain. It was just one of those things. I did it and I was sorry, but I knew I had to put it behind me. But I couldn't, because Rick had seen me at the house that day and had put two and two together. He knew it was me that killed her, and he was blackmailing me, the rat. He said he had the proof that I was there—proof on tape—and he was going to tell the newspapers! Don't you see that would have ruined everything? I had to kill him." Bryan's Adam's apple bobbed convulsively. "He set that booby trap in the bathroom for me. 'No problem unless you've got a guilty conscience,' he said. Right there in front of all of you! He wasn't afraid of me. He thought I was too much of a wimp to get back at him, but he was wrong. Elizabeth was wrong, too. I can kill people if I have to. Now I've got to kill you. But I think it would be better if you had an accident. You and Dusty both. Have you noticed how many people die in careless cooking fires?"

Keeping the gun trained on Meg, Bryan backed up to the work island where the kitchen stove was. With one hand he loosened the lid on the jar of cooking oil that sat on the stove. It was a strange parody of a domestic scene. Bryan carelessly poured cooking oil into a pot with one hand while the other held a wobbly pistol trained on Meg. Oil streamed over the edges of the pot. He tossed the empty plastic container behind him, and with a swift flip of his hand he turned the burner on under the pot. Meg saw the flames from the stove leap to life, blue under the pot. The flame met the spilled oil, leapt up, blackened the sides of the pot, and sputtered down again. "Lots of times," Bryan began conversationally, "people leave a pot of fat on the fire, and the whole house burns down. Happens all the time. Of course, I'll probably help it along a little with some kerosene I've got in the car." He reached out and jerked at the kitchen curtain until it flapped loosely. He pulled a curtain over toward the pot and dipped it in the oil. He smiled. "Yup, we'll have a merry little blaze here in no time. But don't worry. You aren't going to burn to death, Meg."

"Don't shoot me, Bryan," she pleaded. "Please don't shoot me. I won't tell anybody."

"I'm not going to shoot you. Not if you behave yourself. I'm just going to knock you out like I did Dusty. And don't worry. You'll just go to sleep and not wake up. Folks almost always die of smoke inhalation before the fire gets to them."

To Meg's horror a bright crumb of fire appeared on the trailing kitchen curtain, and a bit of the curtain crumbled into blackness as a small trail of fire crept higher onto the fabric.

Bryan slowly edged around the kitchen counter and moved closer to her, keeping the gun trained on her. "It was easy to shoot Rick," he said. "He was so drunk, he wasn't worried, not even when he found out there was a gun at the house at the reservoir. Anybody with a dab of sense would have started to worry then. But not old Rick. He was practically blotto. It was easy to get him to turn his back on me right where I could take aim. I took all the beer out of the fridge and hid it under the kitchen sink." Bryan laughed. "Then when he said, 'What happened to the beer?' all I had to say was, 'The extras are out in the shed.' The stupid idiot put on my raincoat and headed out back. Easy. I just put on kitchen gloves and shot him. But I've shot too many people now." He frowned. "This time it's got to be an accident. That way nobody will suspect a thing. Dusty suspected me, but he's going to be out of the picture. With you two gone, I'll be safe. Everybody'll think Dusty did it, and he'll be dead. Case closed."

Meg could see a dark plume rising from the cooking grease. She had never seen oil get that hot before. It must be almost ready to burst into flame, she figured.

Bryan moved toward her. Meg was so mesmerized by the sight of the approaching gun muzzle that she froze. Just then Bryan's eyes flickered. "That's the tape!" he cried. "That's Rick's tape!" Meg followed his gaze to the tape lying on the couch. "C.C. told me you had it. Hand it here!" he commanded her.

Meg backed up slowly to reach for the tape. When her fingers tightened around it, she hefted it and threw it. Bryan dodged away and the gun went off, exploding almost next to Meg's head. She ducked but wasn't hurt. Bryan had slipped and fallen to the floor and was on his hands and knees struggling to get up. The gun lay a couple of feet from his left hand. Meg tore past him, grabbed her mother's heaviest iron skillet, and banged him hard on the head. Bryan fell flat to the floor. Savagely Meg kicked the gun away from him. To her relief it didn't go off again, but a sudden loud crash from the foyer set her trembling.

"Meg?" Dusty stumbled into the kitchen. "God," he said thickly. "My head is killing me."

Meg laughed shrilly, moved back, and turned off the kitchen burner. "Don't step on Bryan. He's beside the counter."

"My God!"

Meg viciously tore the kitchen curtains down and turned on the water in the sink to soak them. She could hear Bryan groaning. "Maybe you'd better hit him again with the frying pan."

Dusty fingered his head warily. "Are you out of your mind, Meg?"

"Probably," she said. She circled the counter and looked down at Bryan suspiciously. "The soles of his shoes are shiny. I'll bet he slipped on that oil he spilled."

"Well, don't you slip on it," warned Dusty.

"Don't worry." Meg shivered. "Can you do something with the gun, Dusty? I'm afraid to touch it." Slowly she became aware of a siren wailing outside.

The sound grew louder until the klaxon was sounding right beside the house.

Dusty parted the curtains on the door to the carport and peered out the window. "It's the cops!"

Then Meg burst into tears.

17

What I don't understand is how the police got to your house so fast." C.C.'s gypsy earrings swung as she licked her ice-cream cone.

"They could hear everything that was happening on the speaker phone," explained Meg. "I was trying to get through to the police, and when they put me on hold I just left it on so I'd be connected when I got through. It turns out the police dispatcher heard everything."

"Jeez!" said C.C. "That was convenient."

Dusty grinned. "Meg did okay without the police. When I came to, old Bryan was laid out on the kitchen floor like a flounder."

Meg shuddered and glanced around the refreshment pavilion at the mall. Even though Halloween was barely behind them, the mall was already decked out in twinkling lights, hoping to get shoppers in the Christmas buying mood. Families with strollers and sticky-faced toddlers were sharing pizzas. An old lady pushed her husband's wheelchair up to a table and went to get him a plate of food. It was a beautiful, peaceful scene, and Meg could hardly believe that she used to complain there wasn't anything to do in town. It was going to be a long time before anyone heard her say her life wasn't exciting enough.

"He obviously knew you were onto him, Meg." C.C. flushed. "I guess I shouldn't have said anything to anybody about you trying to find the murderer, huh? But gee, I never dreamed Bryan was the murderer!"

"Me either," said Meg bitterly. "Some Nancy Drew! All the time I thought it was Roxy. And don't worry, C.C. You weren't the only one who spilled the beans. I expect Angela let him know I was on his trail, too. You know how chummy she is with Kristin."

"Here come Roxy and Jeff." Dusty eyed them sardonically. "Anybody'd think they were stuck together with Super Glue."

"Roxy's not so bad," said C.C. "And look on the bright side—Kristin's been sent to bed on a doctor's advice, and we haven't had to listen to her for a whole week."

"Hi, gang." Jeff gave them crooked smile. "I guess you're all wondering why I asked you to meet me here. The answer is volleyball! Last one out on the court is a rotten egg."

"Yeah, sure." Dusty pulled out a chair for him. "Just the guy we've been waiting for. What's the latest from the police?"

"Strictly off the record," said Jeff, "they've got Bryan all tied up. The police dispatcher heard his confession on the speaker phone Meg so conveniently left open. And of course they've got Rick's demonstration tape that shows Bryan's car parked at Dusty's house on the day Elizabeth died. Plus his fingerprints are all over the gun he tried to kill you with, Meg. Dad says the only thing left for his lawyers to try is the insanity plea, and nobody gets far with that in this state."

"Elizabeth always used to say Bryan was completely under his father's thumb," said Dusty. "She didn't know how right she was. I can't believe that creep was willing to kill four people to keep his father from being mad at him."

"I guess he knew his father would completely freak out about any kind of bad publicity with the election coming up."

"Well, he's got plenty of bad publicity now," said Dusty.

"Bryan might actually have gotten away with killing Elizabeth if Rick hadn't seen his car there," said C.C.

"Yeah, but it was Dusty's murder party that really broke the whole thing open," said Jeff. "Things happened so fast once we got to the reservoir that I figure Bryan was bound to make a mistake. He was just improvising, making it up as he went along."

"If only I had known it was Rick that had set up that bathroom booby trap," said Meg. "Then I could at least have figured out that he was blackmailing Bryan. But I thought you had done it, Dusty."

"I could have told you I didn't do it, except I didn't even know about it. Nobody told me."

"Where were you when it sprang?" asked Jeff. "We looked everywhere."

"I was on the back porch trying to hear what was going on. I'd planted clues all over the house, so naturally I was waiting to get everybody's reaction."

"I never did figure out the point of that party," said Jeff. "I was starting to think you had cracked up."

"Dusty was trying to make the murderer crack up," said Meg.

"Yeah. Of course, I knew I couldn't be everywhere at once. That's why in the scavenger hunt I paired off everybody I suspected with somebody I thought I could trust. I put you with Bryan, Meg. Then C.C. with Kristin, and Jeff with Roxy. That way, if anybody broke down and confessed, I'd have a witness."

"You suspected me!" cried Roxy indignantly. "I like that!"

Jeff put his arm around her. "He doesn't know you the way I do, cupcake."

Roxy reddened, remembering how pleased she had been when Elizabeth had suddenly and conveniently died. She had been feeling guilty about it ever since. Maybe it wasn't so unreasonable of Dusty to suspect her. Probably she had looked and acted guilty the whole time.

Dusty grinned wryly. "My party didn't exactly turn out the way I planned, did it? As soon as I left you and Bryan in the boat house I ran back to the house and stood on the porch steps under the eaves. I had left the living room window cracked just a bit so I could hear what people were saying when they were in the living room, but when you all went running upstairs I couldn't figure out what was going on, and I just about went crazy."

"It's so weird." Meg shook her head. "You put the gun out in the boat house so Bryan would get scared and confess, and all the time Rick had the same idea! He was obviously sending a message to Bryan, letting him know he was going to tell on him. That's why the whispering voice in the bathroom said 'I know what you did, and I just might tell.' "

Dusty looked down at the paper napkin he had absentmindedly shredded. "I still can't figure out why Rick turned out all the lights in the house. I mean, it must have been him."

"He just couldn't resist giving us a good scare, I guess," said Meg.

Dusty frowned. "I still wish I hadn't brought the gun out to the cottage."

"You didn't realize it was loaded," said Meg quickly.

"Poor Rick," said C.C.

"At least he asked for it," said Dusty. "What about Elizabeth?"

There was a moment of awkward silence.

"It's been awful," said Meg finally, "but we've got to put it behind us."

C.C. slurped her ice cream noisily. "I thought you all might like to know that I've decided it's time for me to get a new boyfriend. In fact, I already have somebody in mind."

"Oh, no," groaned Meg. "I hate to ask who."

"Someone very wholesome," C.C. said. "Someone positively boring, he's so wholesome. Someone even my mother would like. Unfortunately, he hasn't noticed me yet."

"Impossible," muttered Jeff.

"I mean he hasn't noticed me in a positive way," amended C.C. "But I have an idea of what to do about that. My birthday is coming up in a few weeks, and I'm going to have a party."

Meg blanched. "I just want to remind you, C.C., that the last birthday cake we had ended up as police evidence."

C.C. grinned. "Don't worry, Meg. Whatever I decide to do, you can be sure we won't be playing a murder game."

Everyone in the refreshment pavilion turned and stared when they broke into loud applause.